The Cowboy and His Angel

Cowboys of Rock Springs, Texas #4

Kaci Rose

Five Little Roses Publishing

Book Cover By: Sarah Kil Creative Studio

Editing By: Debbe @ On the Page, Author and PA Services

Proofread By: Nikki @ Southern Sweetheart Services

Blurb

He's a cowboy pastor. She has big dreams that don't include settling down. Is he willing to risk it all to go after the one girl he can't have?

I'm not running away. I'm running toward the life I want.

William is everything I always wanted.

A man my parents would love. But Greg is who makes my heart race.

One is a driven businessman in a big city. The other is a small town pastor.

One wants me to be a stay at home corporate wife. The other wants me to follow my dreams and wants to be by my side as I do.

The problem?

The one I'm dating isn't the one that wants to make my dreams come true.

But the one I'm dating is the one my parents would have picked for me.

What the hell am I going to do?

To the coffee that kept me going, and the kids that call me mommy.

Contents

Get Free Books!

Would you like some free cowboy books?
If you join Kaci M. Rose's Newsletter you get books
and bonus epilogues free!

Join Kaci M. Rose's newsletter and get your free
books!
https://www.kacirose.com/KMR-Newsletter

Now on to the story!

Chapter 1

Abby

Rock Springs Texas has always felt like home. Ever since my parents died, and I spent time there on Sage's ranch, it's where my heart wants to be.

Don't get me wrong. I'm so thankful to The Rutherford's for taking me in, while I went to school. Some of their kids have become my good friends, and I love the people I go to school with, but it's just not home.

Becoming a midwife, has consumed my life, and this is the first break I'm getting, and of course, there was no other option than to come home to Rock Springs. When I head back to Arkansas after the summer, I start all of my hands-on training, so I figured I should take this break, while I can.

When I see Sage, waiting on me near baggage claim, we have one of those drop our bags and hug each other moments you see on TV. She's the closest thing I have left to family.

"God, I missed you! I'm so glad you'll be here for a few months," Sage says.

"It's all she's talked about for weeks now." Colt, her husband, says, giving me a quick side hug.

"That makes two of us," I tell him, as we head to baggage claim for the rest of my bags.

Once we get both of them, Colt insists on carrying them out to their truck. He's a true southern gentleman to the core.

"Let's sit in the back and talk," Sage says.

"Like hell woman. I have a bench seat, so scoot that cute little ass over here. I'm not driving an hour not being able to touch you," Colt says.

This makes me laugh. Sage and Colt had a rocky start. They dated in high school, broke up, and then life kept them apart for many years before they got their second chance. Now, you can't keep them apart if you tried.

Sage looks at me and rolls her eyes, before turning to get in the truck. Colt holds the passenger side door open for her, and then smacks her butt, as she climbs in.

"I know you rolled your eyes at me. You'll pay for that later," he tells her.

Once I climb in and settle, he closes the door and climbs in on his side. He buckles up and makes sure Sage is too, before pulling her closer to him.

You can see the love these two have. There's no doubt about it. Too bad I don't feel that way about William.

William is what many would deem the perfect guy. He has a great job, and he's successful at it. He treats me like gold and gets along with The Rutherford's. They love him and like my friends. He goes to my church, supports me going to school, and my visit here this summer. He's everything my parents would want for me. My mom hinted at it many times, and both Mom and Dad thought the world of him. He would visit his aunt and attend our church with her. Though he's everything I should want, I feel nothing for him.

When he holds my hand, when he kisses me, or even when we talk about the future, I feel nothing. Nothing. I might fool myself into thinking I'll grow to love him, but I know that's not true when there's another man, who makes my heart race with just a glance my way.

I want to love William. I do, I really do. I think he's a great guy and will make a great father one day. So, I hope some time apart will make things clearer.

"We're going to church on Sunday. You are coming with us, right? Pastor Greg needs some help with the summer carnival, and it might just be up your alley," Sage says.

Damn.

Just the mention of Pastor Greg has my heart racing. I haven't told anyone how he makes me feel, and I need to get it together in front of Sage and Colt.

"Yeah, it would be fun to do something other than study this summer," I tell her.

For the rest of the drive, she updates me on what has happened, since the last time I was in town. I was here for Christmas, when Sage's brother, Blaze, and his wife, Riley, gave birth to their daughter, baby Lily. Not to be confused with Riley's best friend, Lilly.

After I left, Riley's best friend, Lilly, married her now husband, Mike, and started rescuing horses that have been showing up from what the cops believe is an illegal rodeo.

Sage's other sister-in-law, Ella, had her sister get engaged, and her brother wound up married in Vegas. Sage's sister, Megan, also had her baby girl, Willow.

It's not until she starts talking about how the church ladies are still wanting to get Pastor Greg set up with someone, that I don't really want to talk anymore. Thankfully, this is also when we're pulling into the ranch.

I always loved this place. Several years ago, they expanded and bought the ranch next door, so most of Sage's siblings live on one side, while Sage's parents still live in the main house on the other side, and they run the whole ranch together.

The main house on this side has always been called Sage's place because it's her biological family's land. That's the main reason they bought the place and remodeled it. It's huge too with fourteen bedrooms and nine bathrooms, and that includes two master bedroom suites. One on the family side, and one on the guest room side. There's also an entire housekeeper's one-bedroom apartment downstairs, but as far as I know, it hasn't been used for as long as I have known Sage.

"So, you have three choices of where you can stay. We have the senior ranch hand cabin open for the summer, you can stay in the housekeeper's apartment downstairs, or the guest master bedroom upstairs," Sage says.

"Take the master bedroom," Hunter says, as he and his wife, Megan, come out to greet me.

"Okay, that's fine by me," I say, while Colt and Hunter take my bags upstairs, and the girls pull me into the kitchen.

It's a full half hour of updating Riley, Sage, Megan, Ella, and their other sister-in-law, Sarah, on my progress with school.

By the time I make it upstairs to unpack, I'm exhausted, and I still have to head back down for dinner.

As I finish unpacking and lay down on my bed, my phone rings. When I see it's William, I cringe. I should have called him, when I touched down in Dallas a few hours ago, or when I got to the ranch over an hour ago.

He's video calling me, so I sit up and fix my hair really quick before I answer.

"Hey, there. I wanted to make sure you got in okay." He says with a smile.

There's no doubt about it, he's a handsome guy with his chiseled jaw and perfectly styled brown hair. He's skinny, clean cut, and has a smooth baby face.

It's just the complete opposite of Pastor Greg, who looks like a cowboy, has a hard body with rippling muscles from helping people around town, and is rough around the edges. He's always in jeans and a nice button-down shirt on Sundays, and a flannel shirt the rest of the week.

Damnit, why am I thinking about Greg again?

"Yeah, sorry I didn't call. I just got to my room. Everyone was here and wanted to talk soon, as I walked in."

He gives me a soft smile that I've seen fluster other women. "I figured as much. Sage pick you up from the airport?" He asks, propping the phone up while removing his suit jacket and rolling up his sleeves. He must have just gotten home.

"Yeah, and her husband, Colt. They filled me in on everything I missed on the way here, and as soon as I walked into the house, everyone wanted to know about school and you."

That makes him smile again. "You worked hard at school, and you deserve this break with your friends. I'll miss you like crazy, though."

"I know, but you know what they say about distance and the heart." I try to joke without lying to him.

I don't want to say I'll miss him when I'm not sure if I will. I watch for a sign that he picks up on it. His smile dulls only a fraction before he nods his head.

"Yeah, I've heard that, and I guess we will see, huh? You having dinner with them tonight?"

"Yep, family dinner every night is mandatory. I swear, they're like one of those 1950s families that sit down to eat together, no matter how busy it is. Honestly, it reminds me of my parents." I tell him, putting on a fake smile.

"Okay, I think I'm going to go to my mom's for dinner tonight, so text me, before you get to bed," he says.

"I will. Enjoy dinner with your mom."

"Talk soon." He hangs up.

I flop down on the bed again. I want to make my parents happy, and it's why I agreed to the courtship with William. The church my parents attended wasn't great, but they did believe in courtship, and my parents supported that, as do The Rutherford's.

Courtship means all my dates with William have been with a chaperone. The more I've been on my own and around Sage's family, the less of a fan of courtship I've become, but it's what my parents would have wanted for me. Just like I know they would have wanted William for me. My mom liked him and always said as much.

I'm about to get ready for dinner when there's a knock on my door.

"Come in."

Sage peeks her head in.

"Got a minute?" She asks, closing the door behind her.

"Of course."

"Okay, Colt told me to mind my own business, but you're one of my best friends, so I'm going to say this, and I promise to drop it unless you want to talk about it again. Just know I'm always here, and no judgment ever."

"Oh, for cheese's sake, just spit it out," I say the phrase my momma always said to me that made me laugh. It buys me time to regain my thoughts.

"I don't know William, but I do know you, and I just don't see that spark there. I don't want you to settle. Settling kills your soul. I want you to fall head over heels in love, and find someone who you can't live without. Find the someone who you would have turned this trip down for because you didn't want to be away from him."

I sigh, "It's nothing I haven't already been thinking. Though, I was hoping this trip would provide me with a bit of clarity. I'm not ready to talk about it just yet."

"Well, when you are, you can talk to me, or I can call a girl's night, and you can spill your guts over margaritas, chocolate, and tacos, and then get all of our opinions. It's up to you."

I stand and hug her. "Thank you. Now feed me."

That seems to break the tension, and we head downstairs.

I'm used to family dinners like this with The Rutherford's. Only here, I feel more at home. I'm part of the conversation, I know who they're talking about, and time flies. I don't want to get up from the table. At The Rutherford's, I don't know anyone they talk about, and I wrap up dinner as quick as I can. Such a night and day difference.

Later that night, when I'm back in my room and laying on the bed, I text William.

Me: Hey, I'm heading to bed. Will be up early for church tomorrow.

William: What's the church like there?

Though we go to church every Sunday, and the church there is good, I love the one here in Rock Springs so much better.

Me: It's a small country church, and everyone knows everyone. They're putting on a summer carnival, and I agreed to help.

William: That's what you used to help your parents with. You'll have a lot of fun, and I can come down for the weekend and see the final product.

Me: Yeah. Plus, Rock Springs may be small, but they throw some events that will put Little Rock to shame.

William: Make sure to send photos. I'll let you get to sleep. Talk tomorrow.

Me: Goodnight.

Mom, dad if you are listening. All I need is a sign. One little sign.

Chapter 2

Greg

Another Sunday and another day of the church ladies trying to set me up. I'm a young pastor who is unmarried, so I expected this when I came here. But it seems, the longer I'm unattached, the harder they try to find me someone. Unfortunately, the lower the bar gets set, too.

This week, they're talking about a few girls from Dallas. They have given up on local girls now.

"What about that Erin girl we met over in Lake Worth when we were helping with the charity drive?" Joy Miller asks.

"Oh, yes. She was very sweet and loved helping organize the tables." Donna Norwood says.

"Mom, stop encouraging them," Hunter says, as he walks up with his wife, Megan, who is holding their daughter, Willow.

I'm thankful for the break in the matchmaking. "Why don't you go get your seats, as we'll be starting soon?"

As the church fills up, I excuse myself to prepare for my sermon.

My dad says they wouldn't try so hard to find me a wife if they didn't like me, so I just keep telling myself that. I love it here in Rock Springs, and I hope to be the pastor here for a good long while.

This is the kind of church every pastor wants because you're here for life, but hardly any get it. Few of these spots ever open up, and how I was blessed enough to snag this spot I'll never know.

As I'm heading back to the office to get the rest of my notes, I see her.

Abby.

I heard she was coming back for the summer. She's one girl I wouldn't mind getting to know better, but she's not always living here. My heart races, when she's near, and she's the one person who can make me completely lose my train of thought. I've never had anyone do that to me before.

Right now, I know she's finishing up her classes, though I searched online to find out what her next steps are. Apparently, she has to work with some other midwives and get hands-on experience. There definitely aren't enough people here to train her in our small town.

When I go to the pulpit, the room quietens down. I go through the regular weekly announcements about volunteers for the summer carnival, who have asked for prayer requests, and some of the events in town. Then we sing, I give my sermon, and it all goes by in a blur. Why? Because all I see is Abby. She looks like an angel sitting there in her summer dress with her dark brown hair in a braid over her shoulder.

She's sitting with Sage and Colt, Megan and Hunter, and their parents. They are always a reminder of what love can do for a person. Colt was very much a playboy, and while I don't know the details, I know that's what was said in town. I never saw him set foot in the church. Then, he and Sage got their second chance, and for her, he started coming every week. Now, he's one of my go-to guys, whenever I need help to fix something around here.

Once service is over, I stand by the door and greet everyone, thank them for coming, and chat with whoever stops. The entire time I'm keeping an eye on Abby, who is surrounded by the church ladies. Sage is by her side, so I know she won't let them overwhelm Abby.

When I remember the first time Sage brought Colt to church, and they attended the potluck, a big smile spreads across my face. After Mrs. Dorothy Carey tried to stick her nose in, like Colt didn't belong here, Sage put them all in their place and has walked around on Colt's arm with her head held high ever since.

The next week I gave a sermon on acceptance, and how we can love the sinner, but not the sin. I gave a long speech about how anyone was welcome in this church, no matter their past. Evidently, that was the speech that won Colt over.

I'm so lost in the memory and going through the motions of saying goodbye to people, I don't realize Abby is in front of me until an electric zing shoots up my arm when she shakes my hand.

"Thanks for the sermon. I think it's just what I needed." She gives me a blinding smile.

What the heck did I give a sermon on today? I search my thoughts. Okay, now I remember. It was on how following scripture doesn't mean you have to do things that make you unhappy. It was more directed to the church ladies, as a subtle hint to lay off the girl hunting for a while.

"I'm glad. I heard you're here for the summer?" I ask, wanting to talk to her, even just a bit longer.

"Yeah, I have a break in classes and missed Sage and her family, so I figured it was the perfect time to come visit. Sage signed me up to help with the summer carnival, so you'll be seeing a lot more of me. I hope you don't mind."

Mind? I'm looking forward to it.

"Sage said you had experience putting on some events with your parents' church?" I ask.

Her face clouds over for just a moment, and I assume it's at the mention of her parents, who passed away last year. But the look is gone so fast.

"Yeah, my mom was always involved, and I helped her a lot."

"Well, I might make you my wingman then. Donna Norwood, Hunter's mom, normally helps take the lead, but with Megan just having the baby, she has taken on fewer duties, so she can spoil her grandbaby."

"I'd like that. I'm here to help any way I can."

Oh, boy, don't make promises like that you can't keep. I'll invent ways to keep you near.

"Would you like to get lunch at the diner today and go over what needs to happen? I'm just in the planning stages." I ask. It slips out before I get a chance to stop it.

"Oh, well," she pauses and looks over at Sage and Colt.

"Afterwards, I can drive you back to the ranch. I haven't been out there in a while, so I'm long overdue for a visit." I tell her.

"Only if you're staying for dinner, Pastor." Sage's mom, Hellen, says without missing a beat.

"Well, what kind of pastor would I be, if I turned down a good home cooked meal?" I ask.

I turn back to Abby. "You're welcome to wait in my office. I should be done here in about thirty minutes."

After I direct her to my office, I don't think I've rushed through the end of church so fast before. I peek my head in at the event hall, where the after-church potluck is happening, and give my apologies, telling them I hate to miss it, but I have a meeting for the summer carnival. That makes the ladies happy, and then I'm on my way back to my office.

Entering, I find Abby reading a book from my bookshelf. I see all my notes in the margin, and I know it's the one I got when I graduated from seminary. It's full of testimonies and sermons from many different pastors and priests around the world.

She's lost in reading and doesn't notice me at the door, so I take a moment to watch her. Her dark brown hair is done up in a braid over the top of her head and over her shoulder, and her simple gray dress with white lace hugs her trim figure and looks beautiful on her. Already her floral scent is filling my office, and I hope it never fades.

"I can't tell you how many times I've read that book," I tell her, and she jumps a little before she smiles up at me.

"I'm sorry. I saw the book and wanted to read your notes. My dad had this book, and he did the same thing with notes in the margins. I have his copy and read it often."

"You're welcome to borrow it and read it, if you want," I tell her.

"If I want to read the book, I'll do so here. There's something about reading this book in church," she says.

I get that it feels more meaningful. It's why I keep the book in my office and not at my house.

"Ready to eat?" I ask.

I lead her out the side door of the church to my truck. I normally like walking down to the diner, but the church is on the far edge of town, and it's a twenty-minute walk for me, and Abby is in heels and a nice dress.

When we arrive at the diner, I get lucky and grab a parking spot out front, since most everyone from church went to the potluck.

Walking into the diner with Abby gets me a few looks, and Jo, the diner owner, raises an eyebrow at me, but doesn't make a fuss and doesn't ask any questions.

Once we have ordered, Abby smiles at me, and I swear there isn't anything she couldn't ask me right now that I wouldn't say yes, too. I have to shift in my seat to get a bit more comfortable because I'm getting hard just sitting across the table from her.

"I heard some of the ladies talking before church. They seem pretty determined on setting you up with someone." She says with a twinkle in her coffee-colored eyes.

I just groan. "They are. My dad says I should be flattered because that means they like me, but sometimes, it's a bit much. Though, I think I've mastered how many dates I have to go on to keep them happy. I don't have the heart to tell them all the blind dates are horrible and not just for me. It's easy to see the girls don't want to be there either. Being a pastor's wife isn't for everyone."

"I can't imagine anyone going on a date with you and not having a good time." Her face flushes a pretty pink, and she looks away like she can't believe she just said that.

I can't believe it either. For a brief moment, I think about asking her out, but I stop myself. We're out to lunch now, and she will be around more, setting up the summer carnival, so I need to let things happen naturally if they're meant to happen. After all, I have to practice what I preach.

"So, how is school going?" I ask her when our food arrives.

"Well, so far, it's been all bookwork. I've been working with a midwife up there and assisted in many births, but the real hands-on experience starts when I go back in the fall. That's what I'm looking forward to the most. Being part of a parent's special day."

The joy and energy on her face tells me everything I need to know. She not only enjoys it, but it brings her happiness, too. This is what she was meant to do.

"So, Sage said you have experience with planning events?" I ask, trying not to mention her parents. I didn't like the sad look on her face when I did earlier.

"Yes, my mom and dad were big in our church back home. It's just outside Memphis. The church put on large events to pull in people from the city. Plus, my parents owned and ran a bed-and-breakfast, so we did a lot of weddings and charity events, too."

"Did you all live in the bed-and-breakfast?"

"Yeah, we had a separate part downstairs with our rooms. It had a door that was locked all the time, but an intercom the guests could use after hours. We had a guest room there, too. That's where Sage ended up staying when she was with us. She's like the sister I never had." A smile ghosts her face.

"I felt bad the day I had to tell them I didn't want to run the place and wanted to be a midwife. They were elated and told me they were completely okay to sell the place. When they died, it was an easy transition, because they had started to look into retirement and selling the bed-and-breakfast."

The smile is gone as she pushes her food aside.

"Sorry, I didn't mean to over share," she says.

"One thing I've learned is talking about things is the best way to heal. Sometimes, little things like this are what you need. I hope you'll consider me a friend, so it's never an over share." Damn, I hope I didn't just unintentionally friend zone myself.

She nods her head but still doesn't look back up at me, so I know it's time to change the subject.

"Listen, I know you're here to spend time with Sage's family, but would you consider being my right hand for this carnival? Since Donna is stepping down this year to spend time with her granddaughter, no one has stepped up."

I don't bother telling her I haven't asked either, since I knew she was coming to town.

"Yeah, I'd like that." She says, finally meeting my eyes again.

"Okay, well, want to meet at my place for lunch tomorrow and we can start making plans? I have all my paperwork there."

"I'll be there."

My heart skips a beat. I know it's not a date, but I don't care, because it's not going to stop me from treating it like one.

Chapter 3

Abby

I pull up to find Greg's place is towards the back of the property that the church sits on. Sage let me borrow one of the ranch trucks after I assured her I'd rather go to the meeting alone.

I told her there would be lots of planning to do, and I didn't want her waiting in town for me. Even though I doubt she believes me, she didn't push the issue. I know I want to be able to spend some time with Greg alone today, even if I really shouldn't. Not when I'm being courted by someone else.

As I walk up to the screened in front porch, it's not what I expected. With a summery almost beach vibe, it's all white wood and blue porch furniture.

I knock on the door, and a moment later, it opens, and there's Greg every bit the cowboy small-town pastor in jeans and a flannel button-down shirt that grips his muscles just right. For me, I chose a longer, casual grayish blue maxi dress that's form-fitting up top and loose and flowy at the bottom.

Greg's eyes run over my body, taking me in just like mine do to him, before he clears his throat and steps aside, allowing me to enter the house.

The living room is nothing like I expected. The light gray walls match the blue couch. But unlike the beach theme on the porch, this one is more summer with pops of red and yellow and vases of flowers everywhere.

When I turn back to him, he's watching me and doesn't hide it.

"My sister came into town and decorated it when I moved in. Some of the church ladies bring flowers every week, so I just keep them rotated." He says like he can read my mind.

I notice a family photo on an end table with an older couple, and a woman about his age, who I assume is his sister.

"Definitely not what I expected," I say. "Most pastors' houses on church grounds are old and outdated."

"Oh, it really was, which is why my sister insisted on decorating it. The town was more than happy to have it spruced up. Want the grand tour?"

I nod and try not to stare at his tight, firm butt showcased in those jeans, as I follow him towards the back of the house.

"This is the kitchen and dining room."

The kitchen is a modern farmhouse kitchen with white cabinets and light gray walls. There's a large window that looks out over the backyard. The dining room has a long wood table with chairs on one side, and an L shaped booth under the window on the other side. Great for having a lot of people over, which I'm sure he does.

I follow him back to the living room and down a side hall.

"It's a four-bedroom house. On this side, there are three guest rooms." He walks, pointing to the bedrooms. "I've got two guest bedrooms set up and also a home office here."

I peek my head into a very basic guest bedroom with a dresser, bed, and a few decorations. His office isn't too personal either, not like his one at the church.

"My room is on the other side of the house," he says, indicating the small hallway on the other side of the living room.

"Can I see it?" I ask without thinking. "Sorry, that was inappropriate."

"Not at all. Go right ahead, and remember, it was my sister's doing, but I find I really like it."

What I find is definitely not what I expected. The walls are gray, and his bedding is yellow and gray. There are yellow and gold accents across the room. The bed and rest of the furniture is made out of what looks like old barn wood. While you would think it would look feminine, the wood offsets it, and I can see Greg in here.

Clearing my throat, I turn to him. "Something smells good," I say, needing to change the subject.

"I wish I could take credit, but that's all Nick. He has some new food he plans to showcase at the carnival and wants us to have the first taste."

Nick is Sage's brother and Jason's business partner at the bar, WJ's. He's also marrying Jason's wife and Ella's sister, Maggie. That all went down over Valentine's Day, and Sage and Ella were calling me almost every day with a play-by-play of the event. I might not have seen it happen, but I felt like I was there for it.

"I've always loved Nick's food," I say, following him back to the kitchen.

Nick is too talented to be working in such a small town. He's won several awards for his BBQ, but he grew up here, and this is where he wants to stay, even more so now that his fiancé's family is here.

"Oh, go ahead and sit down. Let me grab the stuff from my office really quick." He says and jogs back down the hallway.

I go to the table and take a seat on the booth side. It almost looks like a large comfy window seat, and from here, I can see the whole kitchen. When he walks back in with a few binders in his hand, he just smiles at me and sets them down on the table, and then turns to the kitchen. He takes the food from the oven and brings it over, along with a pitcher of sweet tea.

"Nick said it's a twist on his popular BBQ tacos," Greg says.

We take a minute to eat, and both agree the duo is amazing.

Then, we start going over stuff for the carnival. Volunteer lists and ideas for getting volunteers, and the info for the pie eating contest and bake sale.

"Last time my sister was here, she outed me to Mrs. Willow," he says. "Told her that I could bake, and she got the church ladies to rally together and demand I enter the pie contest last year. I won, but I don't know if it's because my pie was good, or they just rigged it."

I laugh. "Oh, I know Mrs. Willow. If your pie wasn't good, she'd have been here giving you baking lessons herself."

Greg smiles, and I swear I think my heart stops.

"Have you ever done a pie auction with the contest?" I ask.

"No."

"At the events in Memphis, everyone is required to bake two pies. One to judge, and one to sell. Then, the pies are auctioned off after the winner is announced. The winning pie normally goes for a higher price, and all the money goes to the church."

"That's a good idea. Make a note, and we'll talk to Mrs. Willow. She's in charge of the pie contest this year. Though she's announced that she wasn't baking with her great grandchild on the way, but she'd help organize it. I suspect she'll end up baking if I know her. The contest was set to happen a few days before the carnival, so we could do the auction then, too."

I start making notes in the notebook I brought with me.

After that, the conversation veers off to some of the past pie contests, and how serious some of the ladies get. He tells me some story of the ladies trying to sabotage each other, and we're laughing so hard that I almost don't hear my phone ping with a text message.

Like a bucket of cold water, there is William.

William: How did the planning go?
Me: I'm still here. We're adding in a pie auction like they did at your church.
William: Good idea. When is the carnival?
Me: Next month. I'll call you tonight and tell you the details.

I look up to see Greg watching me again. Tucking my phone away, I smile and ask the first question that comes to mind.

"What made you want to be a pastor?"

His smile dims slightly, but he shares his story.

"We went to church every Sunday. I was in youth group and both my parents helped around the church, but I always wanted to play football. I was offered a football scholarship and everything, but then the last game of my senior year, I tore my ACL which was the end of my football career. While

I was healing, my pastor spent a lot of time with me, helping me figure out what to do. It was too late to apply to other schools, and I of course, lost my scholarship. Going the extra mile, he even helped my parents around the house, doing things I normally would, which really impacted me. I just felt called to do what he did. He prayed with me a lot that summer, and that fall, I was in seminary school."

"Where did you serve after seminary?"

"I was lucky to get my church back home, which is just outside Huntsville, Alabama. Then, I was assigned here."

My phone goes off again, and giving Greg a mumbled sorry, I check it again.

William: I'm going to my parents for dinner tonight. If you can, they'd like to video call with you.

Me: Of course, just tell me what time, and I'll sneak away for the call.

William: Does seven p.m. work?

Me: I'll be ready.

I sigh and put my phone away. Maybe, it's a sign, when I like a guy's parents better than I like him.

"I'd say it's a huge sign," Greg says, and I look up at him wide eyed.

"Did I say that out loud?"

"Yeah," he chuckles.

Now, I feel the need to explain.

"Our church shared many of the same values as Ella's Church. Currently, I'm in a courtship with a man my parents would love. The Rutherford's, who I've been living with, love him. He's handsome, successful, has a great job, his parents love me, and he supports me going to school, but..."

"But it doesn't feel right?" Greg asks.

"Yeah, there's no spark. I like his family more than I like him, and then there was his comment about us having kids." I look down at my hands in my lap.

"You don't want to have kids?"

"I do more than anything. It's just... well, I guess William is a bit old fashioned, and he expects me to be a stay-at-home mom with our kids, and only be a midwife occasionally to help out the church. I was so shocked that I couldn't say anything, but I'm not going to school and doing all this to sit on the sidelines and help the church every now and then."

I look up to find him studying me, making my face heat up.

"I can't believe I just told you all that." I cover my face with my hands.

"Hey, it's okay. I'm not going to tell a soul. I'm here for you to talk to." He gently places his hand on my arm.

Our eyes meet, and that spark is there again. The spark I don't feel with William, and the magic I don't think I want to spend my life without.

Realizing his hand is still on my arm, he pulls away and breaks eye contact.

"It's my job after all to listen and offer advice. If you can open up to me like that, then I'm doing it right."

My heart shutters to a stop. Of course, this is his job. There isn't anything special going on. It's all in my head.

"I didn't know your parents, but I'm sure they would want you to be happy above all else. If this guy isn't it, then that's okay, because there are other ones out there. It has to be a fit for both of you to work," he says.

I stand and start collecting my things. "I better go. I've got a video call with William later."

I have to be imagining Greg tensing up at the mention of Williams's name. My head and heart are playing cruel tricks on me today.

Greg walks me out, but I can't get to the truck fast enough. Without looking back, I pull out and head towards the ranch. Once out of town, I pull over on the side of the road and rest my head on the steering wheel.

Maybe, doing the event with him isn't a good idea.

Then, I hear my mother's voice, telling me I need to finish what I started. I gave him my word, and I need to see it through.

I'll finish helping with this carnival and then keep my distance.

I just hope I can hold on to my heart, until then.

Chapter 4

Greg

I'm getting ready to head to WJ's for dinner tonight. Many might think it's wrong for a pastor to be seen at the local bar. Well, for one, it's the only place that serves dinner in town, and two, and I think it's important to be where the people are. The people are at WJ's on Friday and Saturday nights.

More than once, I'd talked with a rancher there who needed help. I'd show up, help them, and then find them in my church the following Sunday. They might not be every week church goers, but every now and then is better than not at all.

On the drive, all I can think about is Abby. I hated hearing that she was in a courtship with some guy. Not just some guy, but William. But I sat there and listened to her talk. I bit my tongue hard, so I didn't smile when she said she wasn't in love with him, or that she liked his parents better than him.

After she told me, she was so embarrassed, and getting to see her flustered was pretty darn cute. I wonder what other ways I could fluster her when I see her again.

I really liked having her in my house today. She fit, almost like she was made to be there. When she asked to see my room, I got so damn hard, thinking of her in there.

Completely inappropriate thoughts for a pastor, but I'm a man. A man who is insanely attracted to a woman, who asked to see his bedroom. There could be no other reaction. I'm just glad she didn't notice.

This carnival just became that much harder to plan. It's one thing to win her over before, but now that I know she's taken, it's going to be that much harder. If today showed me anything, it's that I want a shot with this woman, no matter how crazy it is. Long distance or just this summer, whatever it takes. I think this is the only way I'll get her out of my system.

That thought makes me cringe because I don't want her out of my system. It's been such a short amount of time, but I can't picture the future without her in it.

When I walk in to WJ's, there's some local band singing country music cover songs, the dance floor is filled, and the place is packed. I don't make it but a few feet in before people start talking to me. It's a good half hour before I make it to the bar and sit down next to Ford.

He recently took over his parents' ranch and is good friends with Mike, Lilly's husband. Mike and Lilly have been taking in all the abandoned horses that are showing up in and around town, and Ford's been helping them out a lot, too.

"How are things going at the ranch?" I ask him, as Jason sets down a root beer for me. It's in a glass bottle that from a distance looks like a beer bottle. It's enough to get people to relax around me.

I don't oppose drinking, but I don't come here to drink. I come here to interact with the town. Jason is great at keeping my secret, and he orders the root beer in the bottle just for me.

"I finally got through the books and understand where the ranch is at. My dad didn't have the easiest system. My sister is coming back in a few weeks, and she's going to take his handwritten books and digitize them for me. She has been trying to get Dad to do it for years, and he wouldn't let her."

"It will make your life easier," I agree.

"You two single men are here hogging each other up when there are ladies who are looking to dance! Shame on you!" Mrs. Willow walks over to us and slaps us on the back.

"I promise to get on the dance floor just as soon as I eat my dinner," I tell her, and she nods, happy with my answer, and then she looks at Ford.

He takes her in stride, standing up and extending his hand.

"Would you do me the honor of this dance Mrs. Willow?"

"Oh, you smooth devil. You know I meant someone your own age, but I'll let you spin me around the dance floor this one time."

She practically drags him onto the floor just as my food, which I didn't order, arrives. Jason always has my back, when I'm here, though I suspect his wife has more to do with that than him.

"I just got another call from the company in Dallas," Nick says, as he joins me and Jason at the bar.

"What company?" I ask, taking a bite of my burger.

"This company called us a few times and wants to come out and talk to us about franchising and broadening our brand." Nick uses air quotes.

"We have turned them down several times, but they keep calling," Jason says.

"So, have them come out, and then hear what they have to say. If it's some city guy, he won't last a day out on the ranch, and then maybe, they will drop it," I shrug.

They laugh. "Okay, but if they don't go running, you'll be joining us." Nick points at me.

"Deal," I laugh.

The more competitions Nick wins with his food, the more publicity this place gets, and the more they'll be contacted. Earlier this year, they did a TV special, after Nick's last championship win. Ever since then, tourists from Dallas have been coming down for the day for his food and doing some shopping on Main Street.

The town has been divided on if it's a good thing or not. Everyone loves the money it brings in, but most don't like all the strangers in town.

"Well," Jason goes on. "Sage insists we up our social media presence. I guess, people are posting all the time and tagging us, and we should be sharing those and posting more."

"Neither of us has the time, and neither of our girls has the time either," Nick says.

Ella is pregnant and working part time at Megan's salon, and Maggie, Nick's fiancée, is building her photography business.

"What about Sarah?" I ask, and they both look at me.

Sarah is Jason's little brother's wife and is working on the ranch with them.

I shrug my shoulders. "She's been helping with some social media stuff with the church, and she's pretty good."

"I'll talk to her," Jason nods.

"Megan is good, too. She's been doing social media for Hunter's vet clinic and her salon, but I know she's busy," I mention.

Jason gets a call and heads to his office, and I finish up my food, before turning and facing the dance floor.

That's when I see Sage and Colt walk in, and my heart starts racing, hoping Abby is with them. This doesn't seem like her type of place, but maybe, she would come out with Sage.

They both see me, wave, and then head my way.

"Abby with you?" I try to ask casually, but Colt's smirk tells me he doesn't buy it.

"No, she had a call with William, and then she was going to hang out with the babies to give the girls a date night," Sage says and nods to the other side of the dance floor, where Blaze and Riley are dancing with Hunter and Megan.

That brings up images of Abby, holding a baby with a huge smile on her face. What would she look like after delivering a baby? The image quickly morphs into her holding our baby, and it's like a vice around my heart. Suddenly, I want that more than I want my next breath.

"How did the carnival planning go?" Sage asks.

"What?" I ask, my mind still focused on Abby with a baby in her arms.

She elbows me, and then I notice the big smile on her face.

"The carnival planning at your place today with Abby?" She asks.

I tuck that image of Abby holding a baby away for later, as I try to focus on what Sage is asking.

"It went well. From working with her parents' church, she had some good ideas, like a pie auction. This Sunday at church she's going to work on getting some more volunteers." I tell them.

Our moment where she told me about William is between me and her, and I won't let on that she left upset, but I wish I had her number to check on her. Then, I have a spark of an idea.

"Actually, I forgot to get her number, before she left, and I'd like to go over a few things with her," I say, letting it hang in the air.

Colt is smirking at me again, but Sage's expression is unreadable, as she pulls out her phone and reads off Abby's number to me.

"If you need help with carnival set up, just let me know," Colt says.

"Same goes for me," Ford says, as he steps up.

"I'll take you both up on that," I tell them.

I stay a bit longer, talking to them and a few other guys, before ducking out, when it turns more into a honky-tonk than a place to eat.

The whole way home, I debate about sending Abby a text. It's not that late, and even if she doesn't reply until tomorrow, then at least she'll have my number.

By the time I pull into my driveway, I'm convinced a short text, so she has my number is best.

I go in and get ready for bed, thinking about how to word my text. Once in my sweatpants and white t-shirt, I lay in bed, getting ready to text her. I type and delete four different messages, before biting the bullet and sending one to her.

Me: Hey, Abby. This is Greg. Sage gave me your number. After how things ended today, I wanted to check on you. I also wanted to make sure you had my number for the carnival planning.

I think that's good enough. It's platonic; a reason she has my number, and I'm checking on her, too. With any luck, she'll text me back tomorrow. I don't expect to hear from her tonight.

Abby: I'm okay. More embarrassed that I unloaded on you like that.

Me: I'm here to listen any time you need.

Abby: It's been a long time since I've trusted a pastor enough to talk like that.

She's trying to put the wall back up, and separate me as her pastor, and not a guy she was talking to. Being that she's seeing someone, I'll let her do it if she thinks it will make the next few weeks any easier.

Me: Well, I feel honored. Also, add Colt and Ford to the setup team. They volunteered tonight.

A few minutes go by before she texts me again.

Abby: Done.

I want to keep her talking, so I take a leap.

Me: Sage said you were watching the babies tonight. How did that go?

Abby: Really good. I used to work in the church nursery, but it's been a while since I was around little ones like that, and it felt good. I missed it.

Me: I've thought about setting up a church nursery. Even though we have the space, there's no one to run it.

Abby: If I was going to be here permanently, I'd volunteer. I loved it. Maybe, we could set up a parent's night out.

Me: What do you mean?

Abby: The Rutherford's church offers for a donation, a parent's night out, where volunteers watch their kids for four hours over dinner time to give parents a date night out. There's no set fee, and it's pay what you can.

Of course, she has great ideas like this. It shouldn't surprise me, because she has been full of them already.

Me: That's a great idea. I wonder if we can schedule it over one of the carnival days, so they can go enjoy the carnival if they want.

Abby: See, that's perfect. You could offer free entry to anyone who volunteers for that night. It should be a pre-register, so we have enough food and enough people to watch the kids, too.

Greg: Offer the parents an entry discount that night, too. We can call it Parent's Night Out.

Abby: I love it. You have some good ideas!

Me: WE have great ideas, and we make a great team.

Abby: We do. Goodnight, Greg. See you Sunday.

Me: Goodnight.

Chapter 5

Abby

It's been a long time since I've been excited to go to church, but knowing I'm going to see Greg, I can't wait. Once I check and make sure that I have all the paperwork I need, then I head out to the ranch truck. Deciding to leave earlier than the rest of the family, I have hopes of avoiding some of their questions.

The church is still pretty quiet, when I get there, even with the scattered cars in the parking lot. I head right to Greg's office and knock on the door.

He's sitting at his desk, and as he looks up at me, my breath catches. The way his dark brown hair falls slightly out of place, and his golden-brown eyes focus on me.

"You're early." He smiles and gestures to the chair in front of his desk.

"Yeah, I ducked out, before everyone really got moving. Thought I'd be here, before everyone piled in, and try to get some sign-ups for the carnival."

"That's a good idea. Also, you can stand with me after church, and we can talk to people then as well," he says.

I have a flash of being a pastor's wife. Always at their side, while they greet people, after the service. Then, I picture myself in that spot. Immediately, I stop that daydream and remind myself of William.

Though, the thought of someone else by Greg's side in that spot doesn't sit well with me, either.

"That sounds good," I tell him.

As people start walking in, I mingle, but I still don't know many faces outside of Sage's family, and our group of friends. But Sage takes pity on me and starts introducing me around before we take our seats.

A few people lead songs, and then there's church announcements before Greg steps up to the pulpit. His eyes find mine, and he smiles before he starts talking. My eyes are riveted on him, and I couldn't take them off, even if I tried.

He goes on to talk about how God's plans don't always make sense when we're in the moment.

Then, he holds up a cross-stitch pattern but shows us the back. All the thread is crossed over each other, and there's no sense of purpose to it. The back looks like a mess of string.

"But when we look back at the finished projects after everything through the mirror of things we've been through," he turns the cross stitch over to reveal a beautiful saying that says trust in God. "It all starts to make sense."

I don't realize how much I need this sermon today. There's a plan in place here, but I don't know what it is, and I feel like I'm off track a bit. I know what feels right, and that's being here in Rock Springs, but I'm not sure how to make that happen.

Taking a deep breath, I remind myself I still have two more months, and nothing has to be figured out today.

I listen to the rest of Greg's sermon, and we sing again before service is over. Then, I jump up, heading over to stand next to Greg at the door to talk up the carnival. He gives me a huge smile, but we don't get a chance to talk, as everyone wants to chat with him on the way out.

He introduces me to everyone, and I don't think I could remember everyone's names, but he does. He knows who comes weekly, and who comes every now and then. He remembers what's going on at their ranch, with their family, and what their kids are doing in school.

He's the perfect guy to be the Rock Springs pastor. He fits in here, and everyone seems to love him.

When he introduces me and talks about the sign-up, people listen to what I have to say, because they trust him.

Several places around town donate items for the raffle, and it's a whirlwind, but the volunteer sheets are overflowing by the time we're done.

I follow him back to his office and collapse on the couch.

"We make a good team, you know." He says as he puts his bible and notes away.

"Yeah, I don't know how you remember everyone, and their names, and what is going on in their life. They all started to blur together at the end."

"It takes time. I messed names up like crazy my first year or so here, but it was the fact that I made the effort that they cared about." Then, he turns to me and asks, "Can I take you to lunch, and we can go over the sheets?"

"Yeah, that sounds good." I smile and stand up.

"I'll drive." He leads me out the side door to his truck.

• • • ● • ● • • •

Greg

The drive over to the diner only takes a few minutes, and we make the drive in silence, but it's a comfortable silence. Like the kind you only have, when you're at ease with someone.

The whole time I'm debating if I can convince her to make this our weekly routine, to grab lunch after church. We have to talk about the carnival and keep each other updated, right? It makes sense to me.

Once we park, I go to her door and offer my hand to help her step out of the truck. A simple gesture, but the moment her hand touches mine, the sparks explode. In this moment, I'm absolutely sure that I know this woman is something special. There's no doubt in my soul.

She seems as shocked as I am about the contact, and I send up a silent prayer that she feels it, too. When I open the diner door for her and pull out her chair at the table, she seems surprised. This William guy must be a fool if she isn't used to being treated this way.

Once we sit down and place our order with Jo, who gives me a knowing wink, we dive right into planning.

"So, we can use my house as the staging area. We do it every year. Everything is stored there gifts, prizes, decor, and things needed," I tell her.

"Sound good. We're going to need it with just about every business in town donating something."

"You'll be joining the pie contest, right?" I ask her.

"I hadn't planned on it. My mom was the baker, but I'm not as good as she was." She shrugs and takes a drink of her soda.

"Come on, it's for a good cause. Plus, I'll bake a pie, if you do."

"You can bake?"

"Yes, my mom and my sister insisted I learn to bake if I was planning on being single and running a church."

She laughs, and that is now my favorite sound in the world. I want her to laugh more. I have seen her smile, but laughing like this, I haven't experienced.

"I think I'd like your mom and sister."

"They will love you," I say, not thinking.

When she gets quiet and looks away, I realize my mistake. I assumed she will be meeting them, and the way it was said, made it seem like it was more than friends.

"My sister comes out every year for the carnival. She eats a ton of carnival food and gets so sick. Her husband just takes care of her, because it's the one time of year she lets go and has fun." I try to change the subject and make things right again.

"So, you have been to some of these pie contests. I was thinking, instead of us baking, we should be judging."

"That sounds good."

"What have been your favorite pies?"

Just like that, we're back talking about safer subjects, as we eat. I'm soaking up every word she has to say until her phone goes off. She checks it, and her smile falls.

"It's William." She says and then answers the phone.

I try not to listen, but I'm sitting across the table, and she hasn't moved away.

"Hello. Yeah, church was good. We got a bunch of volunteers to sign up and got some donations for the raffles."

She listens, but her eyes meet mine, and she mouths 'sorry' to me. I just nod and smile at her, as I eat my fries. When a group of teenagers that were eating in the corner get up and leave, the diner quiets down so much, that I can hear William's voice.

"I'm glad you're getting involved in the church. Hopefully, when you come home, you'll get more involved here," he says.

"Maybe after I finish school. I do miss being involved, but school takes up most of my time," she says.

"I miss you a lot," he goes on. "I've been working long hours to take my mind off you and save up some money for us." Her face twists and I don't think she realizes she's doing it.

"Well, I think being here in Rock Springs has been good for me. I've been so focused on school that I haven't seen what's important that's right in front of me."

He's quiet on the other end of the line. Did he pick up on the fact that she didn't say she misses him, too? Because that omission is screaming in my head.

"I just wish you were involved a little more here is all."

"Your church is so big, and I really only know you and The Rutherford's. Here, the church is small, and I know so many more people. It's easier to get involved. I met almost everyone today, and they all knew me and made it a point to make me feel welcome. It's just easier."

"Well, I'll make sure you feel more included when you get home. When will that be?"

"After the carnival next month."

"Okay. Well, I'll call you tomorrow after work."

They say their goodbyes. Then, she takes a deep breath and turns to me.

"Sorry about that. I forgot he said he'd call me after church."

"You don't ever need to apologize. Things here are very casual if you haven't noticed." I tell her.

"It's one of the things I love," she says.

"I didn't mean to eavesdrop," I start.

"Yeah, you did, but I didn't give you much choice sitting here," she smiles.

Being so direct, she catches me off guard a bit, and I can't help but laugh.

"You aren't this involved in your church back home?"

I hate calling Arkansas her home because I feel like she fits better here.

"No, school took up most of my time. If I'm being honest, the church there is pretty big, and it was very much like high school. Everyone already had their friend cliques, and they weren't interested in a newcomer. William has tried, but I just feel like people tolerate me, because we're courting. I don't feel at home like I do here."

"You know, there's a great local school about twenty minutes from here. I happened to notice that they have a midwife course." I say, hoping not to give away too much.

She looks at me with a mixture of shock and something else that I can't figure out before she schools her features.

"You looked it up?" She asks.

"I might have looked when someone mentioned the school this week." I try to shrug it off. "Ella and Megan both went there for cosmetology, but Megan took a business class there, too."

"I've heard that." She says, her eyes studying me.

It's so intense that I can't hold eye contact, so I let it drop and finish up my food. She does the same, and we finish our meal in silence, but again, it's a comfortable silence.

There's now a hard time limit on the amount of time I have with her, and it ends, when the carnival does, instead of at the end of summer. Knowing this, I want to spend as much time as I can with her.

"Care to make this a weekly thing? Check in, and then catch up after church?" I ask.

Her eyes meet mine for the first time, since the phone call.

"I'd like that."

I go to pay the bill, and she tries to pay her half, but I stop her. She looks uncomfortable, and I don't like that.

"It's on the church, as it's a church meeting," I tell her, watching her relax.

She doesn't have to know I paid for lunch myself. That's between me, Jo, and God.

I'm sure He will understand.

Chapter 6

Abby

I just agreed to have a weekly lunch with Greg after church, and I feel a bit of guilt about it. So that it's not a secret, I need to tell William. There's nothing wrong with a weekly meeting to go over the carnival plans. We only have just over five weeks to pull it off.

The short ride back to the church to get my car is quiet, as we both listen to the radio. My car is the last one in the church lot, and Greg parks next to the passenger's side to let me out.

"I enjoyed lunch today," he says.

"Me too."

He gets out and comes around to open my door. There's a moment when our eyes meet that I swear he's going to say something, but he doesn't.

I walk around to the driver's side of the ranch truck, but something under my tire catches my eye and makes me jump.

"Greg!" I call, and he comes rushing over, as I kneel down.

There's a dog laying there. He's thin, dirty, and his hair is matted.

"He doesn't look like he's in good shape," I tell him.

I slowly move my hand to his nose, but he barely lifts his head to sniff it, before lying back down and letting me pet him. It's a Texas summer, so it's hot out. He needs water and food from the look of it.

"Here, let me," Greg says, and then slowly reaches in to pick up the dog. "He looks like a Blue Healer, but his coat is a bit longer. They're popular around here on the cattle ranches."

As he stands, he looks at me, and then the dog.

"While I hold him, you drive my truck back to my house, and we can get him taken care of."

I nod, as Greg carefully climbs in the passenger seat, and I drive the truck down his driveway to the back of the church property.

Once there, Greg takes the dog inside, not caring about the dirt. I know I shouldn't compare, but I know William wouldn't allow the dog in his house. He won't even let me wear shoes inside, because he doesn't like dirt.

I shake my head and focus on the here and now.

"What can I use to get him some water?" I ask.

"I don't have anything, but there's a pie plate in the cabinet by the stove. It has short sides, so he won't have to lift his head too much to drink."

I find the pie plate, add water, and bring it back to the rug Greg laid him on in the living room.

As soon as I set it down, the dog starts lapping up the water.

"Whoa, not so fast, big boy. Don't want you getting sick." Greg looks at me, "I'm not sure what to feed him, but there are some fresh vegetables in the fridge."

"I'll call Megan and talk to Hunter," I say.

I pull out my phone and call her.

"Hey, girl." She answers.

"Sorry to bother you, but is Hunter there? Greg and I found a dog under my car, and we need some vet advice."

"Oh, poor thing. He's right here. Hang on."

"Abby?" Hunter's voice fills the line.

I go over how we found him, what breed Greg thinks he is, and that we have given him water.

"Okay, let me call my dad. Can you get him to the clinic to check him out?"

"Yeah, I think so. But would it be okay to give him a bath? Also, what can I feed him?"

"Don't give him a bath, until we look at him-, because we don't want to stress him out. When you get here, we'll put him on an IV to hydrate him and feed him some special food, so don't worry about feeding him. Keep giving him water in small amounts, but not too much at once."

Getting off the phone, I relay to Greg what Hunter said. Then, a text comes in from Hunter's dad, who is also a vet and lives in town, and it says that he'll meet us at the clinic in twenty minutes.

After we wrap the dog in an old blanket, Greg settles him on my lap for the ride over. Greg drives slowly, so as not to bump the dog, but keeps looking over at me.

"We're okay, I promise." I smile, trying to ease his worry, but he just gives me a tight smile in return.

When we pull into the clinic, he's out of the door and racing over to my side to take the dog from me, and then carry him inside, where Hunter's dad, Hank, is waiting on us.

I tell him everything I told Hunter about how we found him and giving him water.

"He didn't have a collar on?" Hank asks.

"No." I shake my head.

"Okay then, I'll check for a chip. Many times, the rancher won't collar them for fear of it catching and choking the dog, but they will microchip them," Hank says.

He starts looking the dog over, checking vitals-, and then making sure he isn't injured, since we haven't seen him walk yet.

"Alright, I think he's just weak and used the last of his energy to get under your truck and out of the sun. I'll take a blood and stool sample and get him started on some IV fluids. Once he takes the fluids, and I run a few tests here in the clinic, we will know more," he says.

Greg turns to me, and I see the question in his eyes.

"I want to stay with him," I say.

"I figured you would. If you're staying, I am, too."

"Oh, he's a she, by the way," Hank says, making us both laugh.

"Of course, she is," I say, and then pet her head.

She's a bit more responsive now.

Hank gets the IV set up, and then pulls out what looks like a scanner and runs it over her body on both sides.

"She isn't chipped. I can call animal control..." Hank starts.

"No!" I jump up without thinking.

"It's okay," Greg says, resting his hand on my shoulder. "She can come to stay with us. I can get the word out and see if anyone claims her."

Hank and I both look at him when he says she can stay with us.

"She will stay at my place, and you can come over and help care for her." He says, reading the question on our faces.

He says it so nonchalantly, like there's no reason in the world that there isn't an us. Thankfully, Hank doesn't push the issue, so I just nod and turn back to the dog.

"Now, what would your name be?" I ask.

She tilts her head to look at me. She's already more active with the IV fluids getting into her.

"Princess? Daisy? Hope?" I list off some popular female dog names, but she doesn't react to any of them.

"Bluebell?" Greg says, and she jerks her head up to look at him.

"Well, looks like she has a name. A true Texas name, too," Hank says.

Megan and Sage both text me, asking for updates on the dog, so I share it with them, and they pass the news on. After two hours of fluids, Hank lets us take her home in order to keep her drinking and to feed her some special food he gave us. He says as long as we don't stress her out, we can give her a bath and gently brush her coat out.

On the way to Greg's home, Bluebell is a lot more active and responsive, as she lies in my lap and lets me pet her. Greg still carries her into the house though, and we decide to try a bath.

As soon as he sets her down on the floor, she stands up and sniffs around, before climbing into the tub and sitting down, waiting on us.

We both laugh. "Looks like she's a fan of baths," I say.

Kneeling down next to the tub, we slowly wash off all the dirt we can. Though, we have to soap her up three times, before the water finally runs clear off of her. The whole time we're bathing her, our arms and hands are brushing against each other. Maybe even more than needed, at least on my end. Every time, even the smallest touch, sends sparks shooting up my arm and giving my entire body a warm glow.

I'm thankful we're taking our time bathing Bluebell. Even though it's killing my knees kneeling on the tile next to the tub, I like being this close to

Greg, and having a reason for my arm to brush his, and for him to reach around me.

She likes playing with the cup we used to rinse her off, and half an hour later, both of us are soaked, but she's clean and lets me sit on the living room floor next to her to brush her coat.

Greg disappears into his room and comes out in dry clothes and hands me some of his clothes.

"I'm sure you don't want to stay in those, but I don't have a dress. Though I do have these sweats that my sister left here, and she's about your size. This shirt is mine. I can throw your dress in the drier...." He rattles off obviously flustered.

"This is great. Thank you." I stand and take them from him.

I'm used to only wearing dresses and skirts. I'm not against pants, it's just I was brought up in dresses and skirts, and after my parents died, it was natural for me. So, Greg hasn't seen me in anything but dresses, since I've been here.

I go into the guest bathroom, where we just bathed Bluebell, and see Greg has dried it off the best he could. I pull off my best dress and notice my bra is soaked, too. It really should be dried as well, but I've not been braless around other people.

Hesitating, I decide to try to dry it. I take it off and pull on the blue and purple sweatpants, which fit me pretty well. Then, I slip on the gray t-shirt, which is Greg's. It's a little big on me, and as long as I don't cross my arms over my chest, you shouldn't be able to tell I don't have on a bra.

I gather up my clothes, take a deep breath, and step out into the living room. Greg is brushing Bluebell but looks up when I step into the room.

His eyes rake over my body, and in the past, when guys have done that, it's made me uncomfortable, but when Greg does it, I find myself getting wet down there. Not sure what to do, so I squeeze my thighs together.

I didn't think he'd notice, but he does and mumbles under his breath, looking down at Bluebell.

I clear my throat. "Where is your dryer? I'll toss these in."

"Behind the kitchen on the way to the garage." He says, not looking at me.

I hurry over and put the clothes in the dryer. Leaning against it, I take a deep breath and calm myself, before heading back out there. I've never had a guy turn me on this much, and I know I'm treading in dangerous water.

Turning towards the door, I hesitate, before going out there. Then, I take another deep breath and walk out, like nothing is wrong. After taking a seat on the couch, I pull a pillow over into my lap to hug in front of me, like a shield.

I watch Greg with Bluebell, and he's so gentle and doesn't rush brushing her coat out. When she wants a break to play, shift, or turn, he doesn't get upset. He's so gentle and caring, and it says a lot about the type of guy he is. Whoever the lucky girl he ends up with, I know he will treat her like gold.

Then, in the next instant, I'm already pissed and jealous about some nonexistent future girl he hasn't even met. So much so, I don't notice him getting up and coming to sit down next to me, until the couch dips, and he places a hand on my arm, making me jump.

"What's wrong?" He asks.

"Nothing. It's just stupid," I say.

"No, it's not. I want to hear it."

Looking at Bluebell, instead of him, I say, "I was thinking how great you are with her, and that whoever you end up marrying, will be a lucky girl..." I trail off.

He seems to sense there's more, and he pushes. Of course, he does. "And?"

"And I don't know, I didn't like the thought," I shrug.

He gently places a finger under my chin and turns me, so that my eyes are on him.

"Didn't like the thought of me marrying someone?" He says in a soft tone.

I don't know what to say, so I just nod and look down at my lap.

"Then, I guess we're even." He says, which catches me off guard because it's not at all the response I was expecting.

"What?" I ask, looking back up at him.

"I don't like the idea of you going back to William." His tone is soft, but the muscle in his jaw ticks.

We both stare at each other, but neither of us says a word or moves an inch. There's something in the air between us. It is undeniable and unlike anything, I've ever felt.

He moves so slowly, taking the pillow from my hands, and I let him set it on the couch behind him. Without thinking, I cross my arms in front of me, and I can feel the pull of the shirt over my hard nipples. His eyes run over me again, and when they land on my chest, I can hear his intake of breath. When I look down, my nipples are outlined in the shirt perfectly. I drop my arms, and in doing so, I notice the hard bulge in his lap.

He's as turned on as I am. I slowly move my eyes back up to his, and our eyes lock. The rest of the world fades away, and I swear at that moment, if he doesn't kiss me, I might die. He leans in just a little, and I wet my lips, which draws his attention to them, but he lets out a low groan and leans forward just a bit more.

The spell is broken the moment the loud ring of his phone breaks the silence. I jump back and take a deep breath, as he answers the phone.

Burying my face in my hands, all I can think is, oh my God, what is wrong with me. I was going to let him kiss me. When I should be pushing him away, I was asking for it.

I ignore his conversation, going into the kitchen, and opening a can of the food Hank gave us for Bluebell, and then call her name. She comes into the kitchen carefully, still a bit unsteady, and I slowly feed her part of the can.

Greg wraps up his call, and then comes and watches me feed her.

"Abby..."

"Let's not talk about it. Just forget it. It's a bad idea." I say, babbling but hoping he will drop it because I'm not ready for this conversation.

I continue to feed Bluebell in silence. When she's done, I go and get my clothes from the dryer. They aren't quite dry, but I head to the bathroom to change, anyway. I really need to get going, before I do something stupid, like let him kiss me.

When I come out in my clothes, he looks almost disappointed.

"I should get going. I promised to help cook dinner tonight, and I have a call with William later," I say, reminding us both of why this can't happen.

"That was Mrs. Willow on the phone. Megan called her about the dog, and she's helping spread the word to see if anyone claims her."

"Okay, well, let me know. I'll see you Sunday." I say, rushing out of the door.

"Abby." He says in a steady but commanding voice that I haven't heard from him before. It's one that sends tingles down my spine. I turn to look at him but don't say anything.

"You'll see me before then. Count on it."

Chapter 7

Greg

I'm still sitting on my couch, though I don't know how long I've been lost in thought, thinking about Abby. The day's events cross my mind. Seeing Abby turned on, her filling my shirt in all the right ways, and that moment where I was going to kiss her, and then the big man upstairs stepped in via Mrs. Willow to keep me from crossing that line.

She was right to bring up William. I can't step between this, but she can't tell me she doesn't feel whatever this thing is with us. This feeling is something I've never felt before, and I know in my gut I never will again. I want to fight for her, but I need to take it slow.

As soon as I make the decision, there's a knock on the door. I swear God is stepping in left and right with this woman, because this time, He's making sure I give her space.

Opening the door, I find the town sheriff, Shane. He's a Sunday regular with his wife. Miles is with him. He's a state trooper assigned to the area-, dealing with the possible illegal rodeo we've been seeing.

There have been several horses abandoned in our area so far. Three have shown up here at the church, and several at Mike and Lilly's, once they started taking in rescue horses. There was one that showed up at the vet clinic, too.

"What can I do for you?" I ask.

"Can we talk?" Shane asks, taking in my overly casual attire. It's not often you find me in sweats and a t-shirt.

I step back and lead them in. They both stop when they see Bluebell, who sits and cocks her head at them, seemingly checking them out.

"This is Bluebell. She showed up today. I just got done giving her a bath, and she likes to play, hence the change of clothes." I explain, feeling the need to leave Abby out of the explanation.

"Oh, yes. My wife heard directly from Mrs. Willow about this guy and was sure to let me know," Shane says, as they take a seat on the couch.

"Can I get you anything to drink?" I'm still unsure if this is a social call or a business one.

"Actually, we want to get to the point. We have been going over the horses that have shown up in town, and there has been a pattern. If conditions are right, we're pretty sure the next one will be left here at the church," Miles says.

"And you want to set a trap?" I put the pieces together.

"Exactly. Are you willing to help us?" Shane asks.

"Of course. I want these guys caught as badly as you do."

"So," Shane says. "From what we have seen, the horses are only left, when no one else is around. We talked to Sage and Colt, and they're going to have a huge BBQ party at the ranch on July 4th. Jason and Nick are shutting the bar down, and after some persuading, we got Jo to shut down, too. Pretty much every shop on Main Street will be closed."

"They have started to put up fliers, letting people know about the town closing down for the day. Mike and Lilly are going to the BBQ as well. We'll have a sting team at their place as well as here, but we're pretty sure the drop off will be here, because it's easier to get in and out of town from this location," Mile says.

"Okay, so you want me to join the party?" I ask.

"Yes, but we want you to make a big show of leaving. If the dog is still here, take her with you. There can't be anything or anyone left to spook them. We will have cameras and guys hiding in the empty shops around town," Shane says.

"We have Hank, Hunter, Sage, Mike, and Lilly on standby to help any horse that shows up, and over twenty guys who volunteered to give up their holiday to try and capture these guys," Miles says.

"Well, I'm in. Whatever you need," I say.

"We can start with a large announcement this weekend at church," Shane tells me. "Then, we want the word to spread that the town will be empty. We think whoever is doing this has Rock Springs connections."

• • • ●• ● • • •

Over the next few days, the town starts prepping for the largest party it's ever put on at The Buchanan Ranch. They may be the second largest ranch in Texas, but they don't have parties of this size very often.

The planning keeps Abby busy with Sage, while I'm busy here in town. I won't even get to see her at the party, because they have me meeting them at a safe point.

With both the holiday and sting tomorrow, I'm having one hell of a time sleeping. Partly, because I barely even got to see Abby at church this past weekend, and partly, because I keep going over everything in my head.

I nearly jump out of my skin, when my phone goes off.

Abby: Will you be at the party tomorrow?

I hate I have to lie to her, but no one can know I'm helping the sheriff out.

Me: Yeah, I'll be a little late, but I'll be bringing Bluebell.

Abby: I miss her. How is she doing?

I don't think. I just snap a photo of her, lying at my feet on the bed, and then send it to her. When she doesn't answer right away, I think maybe I pushed too hard.

Abby: She looks so comfortable. I miss her.
Abby: And you.
Me: We miss you, too.
Abby: See you tomorrow.

Almost like she knows I need the comfort-, Bluebell climbs up in the bed and snuggles with me, and between her warmth and the exhaustion from the last week, I finally fall asleep.

· • • ● • ● • ● • • ·

"Bluebell, let's go girl. We're missing the party!" I yell as she sniffs around the truck, before jumping in. I head out towards Sage's ranch, but turn right, instead of left at the intersection, and meet at the sting house, where I was told to go to make sure I was safe.

When I walk in, the guys already have treats for Bluebell, and there are dozens of cameras set up over town, around the church, and at Mike and Lilly's.

"Now we wait," Shane says.

We don't have to wait long, because thirty minutes later, a truck and horse trailer drive into town, and sure enough, they pull into the church. Shane is on the radio, giving orders to his men to wait for the guys to get out with the horse before they move.

When they move in on him, it's a sight to be seen. As one, the team goes in and surrounds him. They capture the man without incident and take him to the sheriff's office in town.

"I'm going down to be there for questioning. But stay here, while we gather the evidence we need from the location," Shane says.

Then, looking over to the state trooper that I haven't seen before, Shane introduces him. "This is Garrett. He will stay with you and keep you updated." Once Shane leaves, Garrett and I get to talking. He's married with two kids in college, and his youngest is a junior in high school. He and Bluebell have a good time playing before his phone goes off.

When he hangs up, he turns to me.

"So, the guy we caught doesn't have ties here. He's from Dallas but isn't talking much. Though, he says he knows a guy from here and was told to bring the horses to the church. He won't say anything else, but his prints match two horse thefts in town, so he isn't going anywhere for a long time," Garrett says.

When I'm finally allowed back to the church, Sage, Colt, Hunter, Mike, and Lilly are still there with the horse.

"We can't get her back into the trailer," Lilly says with a worried look, as I step out of my truck.

Before I get the door closed, Bluebell jumps out and heads right to the horse faster than I have ever seen her move.

"Bluebell!" I shout and head after her slowly, so as not to spook the horse.

But Bluebell walks right up to the horse like the animal can't crush her with one stomp of her foot. Then, the horse bends her head down, and they sniff each other. I slow to a stop and watch closely the exchange between the two.

They seem to have a silent conversation before Bluebell turns and walks into the trailer. As if answering a silent command, the horse bobs her head, before slowly walking and following Bluebell into the trailer, while we all stand there slack jawed watching.

Bluebell comes back out and looks at us, like we have lost our minds, and then pads back to my side.

The spell is broken, and everyone moves to secure the trailer and get the horse to the clinic. I fall to my knees and hug Bluebell.

"You're a ranch dog, aren't you? I'm now torn between wanting to find your owner and hoping I get to keep you." I give her a good rubdown.

"Come on, let's go home and spoil you with some treats," I say, heading back to my truck.

I open the door, and she jumps right in like we've been doing it for years. Then, I put the truck in gear, and we head down the driveway to my place at the back of the property.

Once inside, I pull out some steak, cut the T Bone out of it, and wash it up for Bluebell to chew on. Then, I get to work cooking us both a bit of steak, baked potato, and some rolls.

Bluebell sits on the back porch and watches me expectantly, as I grill, and she enjoys her bone. When I stare out at the Texas summer sky, the feeling of loneliness hits me again. Strange, I never felt this, before Abby showed up, but now, I'm feeling it more and more. When she isn't here, I'm not content to be alone, and it feels like something is missing.

She's with William, and there's a reason she's still with him, and I have to keep reminding myself. That reason is for her to understand, even if I don't. I won't get in the way of that, but I can't help but be aware that I have these feelings for her for a reason, too.

Why would I be falling for her like this, or why would we be pushed together like this, if there isn't a reason? I have to remind myself of the sermon I gave about how God's plans don't always make sense, during the process. That sermon was for me more than anyone else, I do know that.

The problem is right now it just hurts. It hurts knowing she's not mine, it hurts when she's around, and I can't touch her. It hurts knowing some other guy has a claim on her. It hurts knowing in a few short weeks she's going home to that guy, and he will get her hugs, kisses, and smiles.

Please, God, I just need a sign. A sign that I'm on the right path, and this is where you need me to be. I send up the prayer just before I pull everything off the grill.

No sooner do I step inside, than there's someone pounding on my door. Bluebell runs to the door, barking and dancing in a circle. I set the plate down and go see who it is.

Damn. God sure works fast.

Chapter 8

Abby

P retty much everyone in town is here at the ranch to celebrate the 4th. The grills are working overtime, and we were baking for days. Everyone brought a dish, and there are games for both adults and kids to set up.

As I walk around, I keep telling myself not to look for Greg. I shouldn't care that he's not here. The longer I go without finding him, the more agitated I get. So, when a text comes in, I jump at the distraction.

William: Hey, do you have time to chat?
Me: Yes, give me a few minutes to go up to my room, where it's quiet.

I excuse myself and head to the main house and to my room.

Me: Ready when you are.

Instead of a normal phone call, it's a video call.
"Hey, there. You look different." He says with a huge smile on his face.
"A good different?"
"Yeah, more relaxed and casual."

"Well, I've been outside all day. It was easier to skip the makeup and throw my hair up."

"I like this look." He winks at me. He's been flirting a lot more lately, and I don't hate it.

We spend the next hour talking about the holiday and catching up on the last few days. I peek out of the window, showing him how crowded the ranch is for the party, and we talk about how the carnival planning is going.

"Everything gets delivered next week, and we're doing the pie contest and auction with a bake sale the week before the carnival."

"Are you entering a pie?"

"Not for the contest, since I'm a judge, but I'll do one for the bake sale and auction. One of my mom's recipes." I say with a smile.

"Well, I hope when you are back home, you'll make it for me to try, too."

"Gives you something to look forward to."

"Trust me, I'm looking forward to you coming home. I miss you, and it's just not the same without you."

"To be honest, I'm torn. I love it here, but I miss my life there, too. It's as if both places feel like home," I admit.

"It's like when you live in one place, but your family is in another. They are your family, so it's natural," he says.

William always knows what to say to make me feel better. The problem is, it isn't any less confusing, even more so than most of the time. We hang up and promise to talk again in a few days.

Instead of going back to the party, I just lay in bed and think of William's words. The problem with his theory is Rock Springs feels more like home than Arkansas ever has.

Finally, I realize I'm probably being missed at the party, so I head back down and run into Megan and Ella in the kitchen.

"Have you guys seen Sage?" I ask.

They look at each other, and then Blaze chimes in.

"They're at the church. Pastor Greg helped set up a sting operation to catch the guys leaving the horses. They caught someone, but the horse that he has is giving them trouble."

My heart sinks. Greg was working with the cops in a sting operation? I may have grown up sheltered, but even I know how dangerous those can be.

When I leave and try to call him, he doesn't answer. Without even giving it a thought, I grab the keys and go out to the truck I've been borrowing.

It takes too much time getting off the ranch with so many people here, but my only thought is getting to Greg. As I drive to his place, I wonder if he's okay. Is the horse okay? What happened?

About the time I get to the main road, I'm mad he agreed to do this and put himself in harm's way. Why didn't he tell me? Why on earth did he do this?

I get to the church, and there's no one there, but the grass is all torn up like something happened. Then, I drive back towards Greg's place and breathe a sigh of relief, seeing his truck in the driveway.

On the walk up to his front door, the smell of the steaks he has on the grill hits me. It makes me hesitate only a moment before I ring the doorbell.

In the house, I hear Bluebell barking up a storm before the locks start clicking, and Greg opens the door. He's dressed like he was going to a party. Dressier jeans, cowboy boots, and a nice button-down shirt.

A quick glance shows there are no marks or bruises on him. Other than some dust on his boots, nothing looks out of place.

I don't know if I should hug him and be thankful he's okay, or yell that he chose to put himself in that situation.

What comes out is a cross between a yell and a cry. "You're o... okay."

Understanding crosses his face, and he pulls me in for a hug and holds me tight, as I start crying.

"I was never in any danger." He whispers into my hair and guides me to the couch to sit down. He keeps me in his arms and holds me tight.

When the tears stop, I realize that I'm snuggled up to his chest, and his arms are around me. I jerk back before I can think of it. These are not William's arms, and I'm way too comfortable in this man's arms.

"I'm sorry." I wipe the tears off my face.

He studies me for just a minute, before hesitantly reaching foreword and dabbing at a few tears.

"I was never in any danger, Abby. They just needed the place empty. I was at the old Richard's place, watching everything on a camera."

I lean into his hand, and our eyes lock.

"Why didn't you tell me?"

"I wasn't allowed. We only told Sage and Colt, so they would have the party. None of her family knew until we called them to come for the horse." He says just above a whisper.

A few more tears fall without me meaning for them to. Greg sighs and pulls me in for another hug. This time running his hand through my hair.

"I wanted to tell you, but I needed you to be safe, and that meant on the ranch with everyone else in case this didn't go as planned. I'm not sorry about that. My only regret is I said I was coming to the party, and then didn't make it."

This time I let him comfort me, and we sit there just soaking each other in.

"Your food must be getting cold," I mumble.

"I don't care about the food." He whispers back and holds me tighter. Then, he goes over the events from earlier, while he holds me and comforts me.

Right now, in this moment, I feel safe in his arms, like he will protect me from the outside world. For the first time in a long time, the pain of losing my parents is gone, as well as wondering what they would want me to do is not pressing on me.

For the first time, since they died, I feel like me again. The me I was when I had them having my back and protecting me. It's not only with Greg that I have that assurance but with being here in Rock Springs as well.

The problem is my school is in Arkansas, and my future job is there too.

Almost like he knew I needed to get out of my head, he chuckles. "You should have seen Bluebell."

"What did she do?" I ask without moving.

"The horse didn't want to get into Sage's trailer, not that I could blame her. Bluebell went right up to her, and they sniffed each other out. Then, Bluebell walked into the trailer, and the horse followed. When Bluebell walked out, she looked at us all like we were crazy for being stunned."

I sit up and look at Bluebell, who is lying on the rug by the front door, almost like she's protecting us.

"Come here, girl." I pat my lap, and she jumps up and runs over to us, leaping into my lap.

She lays half on my lap and half on Greg's, while we pet her, and she looks up, and I swear she has a big grin on her face. As we spoil Bluebell, Greg keeps me close to his side with one arm behind my back and resting on my hip.

It's one of those perfect windows in time my mom and dad were always talking about. Those exquisite moments of everyday life, where everything is just as it should be. A normal ordinary moment that unless you stop and take it in, would pass by in a flurry of happiness and blend into the next.

It's not something I have had in a very long time, and I don't want it to end. What I want is to stay here in Greg's arms and in Rock Springs.

But there's too much to figure out. School, a job, William, and the rest of my life. I can't throw it all away in one moment like this.

Almost like fate is stepping in, my phone rings. Greg and I lock eyes for a moment before I reach into my pocket for it.

William.

If that's not a sign, I don't know what is. I hesitate for a minute, and then send him to voice mail. I never do that, unless I'm in class.

When I look at Greg, a pained look crosses his face, as he's looking at my phone. Yet, when he looks back at me, it's gone.

"I should get going. I didn't really tell anyone I was leaving, or where I was going. I just heard the news and kind of left."

He nods, we both stand, and he walks me to the door. The pained look is back, and he opens his mouth and closes it, pressing his lips into a straight line. I can't take my eyes off his mouth, as my heart races.

"Damnit." He says and then takes a step back from me.

I have no idea what's going on, as I look back up at him.

He leans forward just enough so that we're at eye level "You can't look at me like that. You aren't mine, and I'm trying to be good here. But you have to help me out, and not look at me like that anymore."

"Like what?" I ask out loud, not really meaning, too.

"Like I'm yours. Like you're going to kiss me. Like you're going to be mine."

My face heats, and suddenly embarrassed, I turn and rush to my truck, letting the cool breeze on my skin help me calm down.

"Abby..."

Halfway to my truck, I turn to look at him.

"We're okay. I promise to make things easier on you. I didn't realize..." I just shake my head and give him a forced smile, before turning back and getting in.

I don't look back at him, as I drive down the driveway. I can't, because then, I might do something stupid, like turn around and actually kiss him.

When I get on to the old road leading to the ranch, I pull over on the side to call William back.

"Abby, is everything okay?" He asks.

"Yeah, I'm sorry about that. What's up?" I try to play it off.

"My parents wanted to talk to you before I left, but I'm home now. Are you sure everything is okay?"

I don't want to lie to him, so I tell him about the horse showing up, and Sage, Colt, Hunter, Mike, and Lilly helping out. How when I heard that I went down to the church to see what I could do.

I leave out my time with Greg, but do tell him about Bluebell, and how I took some time to spoil her.

In a soft, worried tone, he says to me, "I don't want you putting yourself in harm's way like that."

"By the time I even heard, they had arrested the guy. So, it was just about getting the horse to the clinic and making sure the church didn't need anything. Part of the yard is torn up, but that is an easy fix. I just wanted to help."

"But I don't want you getting mixed up with this. An illegal rodeo? That can be dangerous, and if they get a glimpse of you, who knows what ideas they might get."

How he says it makes a chill run down my spine. Where Greg made me feel safe and warm, William is putting fear in me. I know it comes from a good place, but the contrast between them both is very different.

"I need to get back to the ranch. I'll talk to you soon."

Then, I end the call and do what I promised myself I wouldn't do. I start comparing the two in my head. Greg knew what I needed, where William thought I had no idea what could go wrong.

William treats me like I know nothing of the outside world. Maybe, it's my fault, because I let him. I know more than he thinks. I don't need him to shelter me and take care of me.

Maybe, I should have told him about the drama with my parents' church, after my parents died. When they tried to steal my parents' estate from me, I was in more danger there. Thanks to Sage and Colt, we got them arrested, but today, was a cakewalk compared to that ordeal.

I didn't talk about that or about my parents' death very often. Sage was there for me, and maybe, that's why I feel this connection to Rock Springs so strong. My mind drifts back to Greg.

It's Greg who treats me like an equal. That's what I want, but the need to make my parents happy is even stronger.

"I need a sign. Any sign." I whisper to Mom and Dad, hoping they hear me.

After I take a few calming breaths and get ready to drive, my phone goes off, letting me know I have a text.

Greg: Please, let me know you make it home safely. I'm sorry I upset you, but I hope to see you on Sunday for our weekly lunch.

Chapter 9

Greg

I 'm so lost in my feelings for Abby. After she left, I spent the rest of the night reading the bible, and in prayer, hoping to find something of comfort, anything to put me back on the right path, but nothing came.

So, this morning, I decided to call my sister. Since we live so far apart, we always do video calls-, because it helps us feel more connected.

"Well, don't you look like hell?" She says, greeting me.

"I've met her," I say, as shock crosses her face.

Her being the girl I'm going to marry; the love of my life. My sister found her soul mate, and I refuse to settle for anything less. For a while now, my sister has been harping on me to find her, and now I have.

"Tell me about her." A huge smile crosses her face.

"She's dating someone else."

"Don't get in the middle of that." She says, her smile dropping, and her voice going cold.

"I'm not. She feels something for me. I know it, but she's fighting herself."

Then, I proceed to tell her about Abby, about the last few weeks, and yesterday, when she showed up worried about me.

"Okay, with that out of the way, and what you have told me, it sounds like this guy is more of a brother or a friend. It also sounds like she's with him because it would make her parents happy, and not because it's what she wants," she says.

"That still doesn't mean you can interfere." Her husband yells from the background.

"I know, but that doesn't mean I can't show her what could be. From what she's already told me, I know she wants to be here in Rock Springs, but there are things holding her back. School is a big one," I say.

"Yes," my sister says. "So, make sure she knows her options while keeping your distance."

"I've told her about the local school. Though I could talk to Riley and Megan's doctor and mention Abby might be looking to, what is it called, intern? I'm not sure."

My sister collapses onto the couch next to her husband.

"Of course, you find her, and she's with someone else. This is going to be one hell of a test for you," she says.

"I know, and I'm going to fail. The other day I almost kissed her. Then yesterday, I held her closer than I should have and admitted more than I wanted, too."

"Maybe, you need to keep your distance a bit. This has to be her choice."

"I can try, but I have a weekly lunch with her to go over the prep for the carnival."

"Then, you know what you need to do."

"I'm getting ready to head to Dallas now. It's why I'm up so early." I tell her.

It's just after six in the morning. It's seven where my sister lives, and they're getting ready for work. Normally, I call when they get home for the day unless something is up like today.

"Go talk to Ian, and I'll talk to you soon," she says.

We say our goodbyes, and I make sure Bluebell goes outside and has plenty of water. I'll likely be gone all day. Mrs. Willow agreed to stop by after lunch, let her out, and check on her for me.

I get in my truck and head towards Dallas. Ian is always the one I go talk to when things get rough. When I need a pastor to talk to, when I need advice, and when I need to pray, he's the man. If there was ever a time for me to pray, then now is it.

Once in Dallas, I stop at the bakery close to Ian's church and get some donuts and coffee for us, because Ian is not a morning person, and I know he's up early for me.

When I knock on his door, and he sees the coffee and donuts, he smiles, and I follow him to the living room. I haven't told him what is going on, just that I need to talk.

We each have a donut and some coffee before he turns to me and gets right down to business.

"What's wrong?" He asks.

"I met my soul mate," I say.

Looking me over and reading me, he only says one word. "But?"

"But she's dating someone else. She lives in Arkansas, and she's going to school there."

"But you can't ignore her... you have already spent a lot of time with her," he says.

"It's scary how much you can read me. Yes, she's in charge of the summer carnival this year, and we're having lunch every week after church."

"At your house?"

"At the diner, but we have eaten at my house once."

"Keep it public and always be transparent. You should try not to be alone with her if at all possible.

She needs to know you have her best interests at heart, always."

"My sister said roughly the same thing."

He chuckles and reaches for another donut. "She's a smart woman. I always liked her."

"I know this is a test, but I'm just not sure if it's mine or hers."

"It's both of yours."

He sits and prays with me, and then we finish our food, as we talk and catch up. I tell him about Bluebell, the horses, and all the church events going on.

"How's your wife?" I ask.

"She's leading the women's mission trip, but will be home next week. The girls love her, and I've seen her touch many lives with that ministry." He says with a smile on his face.

Before I head home, I attend his mid-morning service. Ian taught me about planning sermons ahead of time. So even though I know he planned this sermon a week ahead, when I hear it, I think this one is targeted right at me.

He's talking about the different relationships in our life. Those around us, the ones we have with friends and family, the ones we have with God, and how we treat them today, and how they affect us in the future.

After saying my goodbyes, I stop to grab some lunch, and then some of the fudge I know Sage and her sisters love. Though, I know my excuse for taking it to them to thank them for helping with the horse is flimsy. I know it's to see Abby and to make sure she's okay after yesterday.

I drop the fudge off at my house, before loading up Bluebell and going over to Ford's ranch. He just took the ranch over, so his parents could retire, and I have been stopping in to check on him.

All the ranch hands have stayed on, so the transition has been smooth, but I always like to check in.

As I drive up to his barn, everything looks in order, which is a good sign. He meets me at the barn door, as I pull up, and Bluebell heads right to him, the moment her paws hit the dirt.

"I heard about you, girl. Mike was singing your praises." Ford says, leaning down to pet her.

"Any news on the horse?" I ask.

"Yeah, she has two hairline fractures in her legs and a rib, rain rot, her hoofs are in bad condition, and of course, she was drugged, like the others. But Hunter says she's very lucky and should recover, though there's a good chance she might not be able to be ridden again."

"They can still use her in the camp. She's a good one for brush downs, and all if her temperament is okay."

"I agree." He says, and then nods towards the barn, and I follow him.

"This is my first foal, since taking over. She's got good thoroughbred bloodlines."

"You going to race her?"

"Nah, I'll sell her. The last foal brought in a quarter of a million and has several huge championships under his belt. With any luck, we will get close to that again," he says.

"No reason you shouldn't."

"Best investment my dad ever made was these two horses."

I chuckle. Ford's dad bought these two thoroughbred championship racehorses from a down on his luck owner with a gambling problem-

, who needed some fast cash, after a poker championship in Dallas.

He decided to try breeding them, and the first foal more than made his money back. This is the third foal from this pair, and it's been a great source of money, since then.

"I remember how mad your mom was, when he bought them, too. She was in church angry praying for a week straight," I chuckle.

"Angry praying?"

"Yelling and cursing," I smirk.

"You didn't kick her out for that?" Ford asks a bit shocked.

"I find that's the most honest and raw type of prayer. They also tend to be the most answered." I nod towards the foal.

When Ford makes the connection, he starts laughing.

"I'll keep that in mind." He says, resting a foot on the stall gate, while crossing his arms and resting his chin on them, staring at the little horse walking on wobbly legs.

"You know, I remember the first time I saw a horse born on the ranch. I was eight and asked the stupid question of how the horse got in its mom's belly. I was way too young for the birds and bees talk," he chuckles.

"I don't think there's ever a perfect time for it."

"Very true. Do you have plans tonight?" He asks.

"Nope. You need help with something?"

"No, actually, Mike is dragging me out to Sage and Colt's place. The girls are doing girl's night at the main house, and the guys are meeting at the parents' for a guy's night with cards, food, and that sort of thing."

I should say no and give me and Abby space. In my mind, I can hear Ian shouting for me to say no right along with my sister and my brother-in-law. A stronger man would have declined and went home to have dinner alone.

If this was a test, I failed, because no matter how hard I try, I still hear myself saying, "I was in Dallas and stopped and got the girls some of the fudge they love. It will be perfect for girl's night."

"So, that's a yes?" He asks.

"Yeah, just have to stop home, clean up, and grab it."

"Okay, we're meeting there at six. See you then."

I head home and shower, while I spend some time trying to talk myself out of going, but it doesn't work. I dress up a little, grab the fudge, Bluebell, and I'm back in my truck, heading out to the ranch.

Even though I know I'm supposed to turn the truck around, no amount of bargaining gets me to do it either.

I park at the main house and take a deep breath. Then, I open the door and Bluebell runs out, barking towards the barn. A moment later, Abby walks out in a jean skirt, boots, a flannel shirt, and her hair pulled up over her shoulder, and she's looking like an angel.

When she sees me, her smile is so large and welcoming, that it makes my heart beat hard in my chest.

I'm in so much trouble.

When she walks over to me, I can't find the words to say what I want to her, so I just hand her the chocolate.

"I was in Dallas and picked this up for your girl's night," I tell her.

"Thank you! I've only had this fudge once, and it was to die for. You heading to Sage's parents for guy's night?" She asks.

"Yeah, Ford invited me. I figured it's been a while since I've seen her dad and her brother Mac, that I should come out and catch up."

"It's going to be some kind of night. Mike and Lilly are joining in, along with Nick, Maggie, Royce, and Anna Mae."

"Perfect! I need to talk to Nick and Maggie about the wedding, so even more of a reason to be here." I don't know who I'm trying to justify my visit to more, her or myself.

"Well, make sure you stop by and say goodnight, before your leave," she says.

I run my eyes over her, before giving her a soft smile.

"You can count on it."

Chapter 10
Abby

I promised Ella I'd help her in the garden. With her being pregnant, she can't do all the weeding like she used to, and I don't really have plans, so I figure the least I can do is help out. I'm also hoping it will take my mind off a certain pastor.

Even though I'm not much of a gardener, I can follow Ella's instructions. Things were going great until she mentioned Greg.

"So, how is the summer carnival planning going?" She asks.

"Good, everything is on track, and we have plenty of volunteers."

"Sage said you're having lunch with Greg every week after church to go over plans?"

"Yeah."

"When Hunter's mom was running it, they met once or twice at most," Ella says.

"Well, I'm new, and I've never done this before. So, I'm sure he just wants to stay on top of it, and I can't blame him." I say, knowing what's coming next.

"It's more than that, and you know it." Jason comes out and sits next to his wife, putting a hand over her belly, as if to protect their unborn baby.

"But I have William," I say, hoping it will put an end to this conversation, but my luck isn't that good.

"Abby, I'm going to overstep here, and you'll forgive me because I'm pregnant. But I have not once seen your face light up when you talk to William or about him. Not the way it does when you talk about Greg. I have not seen you as happy and relaxed as you are here in Rock Springs. Though I'm not sure what's holding you back, but whatever you do, don't settle," Ella says.

I mull it over. She put words to the feelings I've had, and it's the first time I've really heard them spoken out loud.

"William is exactly the guy I always wanted," I say, not really believing it myself.

Ella sighs, "You know the church I came from with the courtship and the rules. I knew a long time ago I couldn't marry and spend my life with someone I didn't love, and someone that didn't make me happy. My parents thankfully agreed, and then in walks Jason. He made my heart flutter, and I found it hard to breathe around him. He was nothing like the guy my church would have approved of. Yet, he's perfect, sweet, and treats me like gold. You can't fit love in a box, and when you try, you will just end up hurt."

I turn back to pulling the weeds, trying to not encourage the conversation any further.

"How's Bluebell?" Jason asks, thankfully, ending that line of conversation.

"She was doing so much better the last I saw her. No one has claimed her, and I heard Greg has plans to keep her if no one does. We're shocked she hasn't been claimed," I say. "Because there's no doubt about it, she's obviously a ranch dog with the way she helped get the horse in the trailer."

"Well, maybe you should go check on her. Get some pictures and hang them up at the bar and the diner. Almost everyone in town will see them that way," Ella says.

"Good idea," I say, nodding. Thankfully, the subject switches to tonight's plans. "So, girl's night here at the main house, and guy's night at the parents' house on the other side of the ranch?"

The rest of the day flies by, and Ella calls it a day. We take some stuff into the barn to put it away, and on the way out, I'm pulled from my thoughts by Bluebell, running up to me. Leaning down to pet her, I look up, and my eyes lock with Greg.

Because I didn't expect to see him today, I wasn't prepared, and I can only imagine what I look like, after all day out in the garden. But when our eyes lock, and he smiles at me, none of it matters.

As my feet, with a mind of their own, take me closer to him, my pulse races, and I can't remember any of the reasons I should stay away. When I reach him, he holds out a box to me, and I see that it's the fudge from the place in Dallas that Sage is always talking about.

"I was in Dallas and picked this up for your girls' night." He says

"Thank you! I've only had this fudge once, and it was to die for. You heading to Sage's parents for guy's night?"

"Yeah, Ford invited me. It's been a while since I've seen her dad and her brother Mac, so I figured that I should come and catch up."

Ahhh, yes. Lilly invited Ford tonight. Ford and Mike have become good friends, and I think Lilly has taken it on herself to find Ford a girl. I think she has someone in mind, but she won't admit it or tell me who, so I just let it go.

"It's going to be some kind of night. Mike and Lilly are joining, along with Nick, Maggie, Royce, and Anna Mae."

"Perfect, I need to talk to Nick and Maggie about the wedding, so even more of a reason to be here," Greg says.

I'm kind of excited about their wedding. They got engaged on Valentine's Day and have been planning a big wedding ever since. They had a dual bachelor and bachelorette party in Las Vegas, where Maggie's brother, Royce, ended up getting married to his now wife, Anna Mae.

If you believe the stories, they got drunk and woke up married. Royce wouldn't let her out of it, and they moved in together, and things went from there. They're now expecting their first child.

I make a note to stop by and visit with them, while I'm in town. I'd really like to hear the true story.

"Well, make sure you come over and say goodnight, before you leave," I say.

He runs his eyes over me, before giving me a shy, endearing grin.

"You can count on it."

Those words make my heart flutter again. So, I just smile, nod, and turn to go inside. Setting the fudge on the counter, I run up to my room and collapse onto the bed.

After being outside all day, I let myself catch my breath before I get up and take a quick shower. I do my hair and add some mascara and lip gloss, before picking out a casual but cute outfit.

My plans were to just toss my hair up and be comfortable, but knowing I'll see Greg before he leaves, I want to make sure I look good, too.

As I'm picking out an outfit, my phone rings. It's William. For the second time since I've been here,

I ignore his call and finish getting dressed. Then, I send him a quick text.

Me: Sorry, girl's night, and it's kind of loud here.

William: Just wanted to say goodnight. I have an early meeting, so I'm going to bed early.

Me: Okay, call me tomorrow?

William: Of course, I want to hear all about girl's night.

Me: I've been sworn to secrecy, but I might share a few juicy details.

William: Have fun. Talk to you tomorrow.

Then, I head downstairs to find almost everyone eating the fudge.

"That didn't last long." Shaking my head, I take one of the last pieces.

"Fair game, because it was on the counter. Who brought it?" Sage asks.

"Greg brought it over," I say, watching everyone stop eating instantly and I smile. "It's for all of us."

"Oh, good, because I wasn't giving my piece back." Ella laughs and rubs her belly.

After we all grab a plate of food that Sage and her mom, Helen, cooked and brought over, we head into the dining room.

"You know, I saw you talking to Pastor Greg when we came out of the barn, and the way he looked at you, even I could feel the sizzle," Ella says.

"I'm not denying there's an attraction there, which is what makes things so hard," I say.

"Because of William?" Sage fills in the missing pieces.

I nod, noticing the confused look on the other girls' faces, so I fill them in on William and our relationship so far.

"We may have all found our guys," Sarah says. "Though, it wasn't an easy road. But I know I can say in my heart, I knew Mac was the one, yet I wasn't willing to admit that at the beginning."

Anna Mae joins in, "Royce knew almost instantly I was it for him, but it took me over a year, an accidental Vegas wedding, and almost losing him before I realized it."

"You know, Colt and I knew, when we were six, we had something. Then, in high school, we knew it was love. But I got scared and ran, taking us years to find our way back to each other."

"Yeah, I know your story. We've spent many nights up talking about it," I tell her.

That's how we met. She stayed at my parents' bed-and-breakfast. Then, when my parents were in a bind, she stayed to help us out. That led to many long nights of staying up talking, and we often ended up discussing her and Colt.

It was still a while after she left us before she went back to him. But I'm so glad she did because the love they have is one like what my parents had. The kind I want.

"But William is exactly the kind of guy my parents would want for me," I say.

Sage gets up and crosses the room to sit next to me.

"I didn't know your parents long, but it didn't take people long to see that your happiness meant the world to them. It's why, when you wanted to be a midwife, instead of taking over the B&B, they didn't even bat an eye."

"My mom always said, when you meet the one, you'll know, because suddenly, you can't see your future without him in it," Maggie says.

"I remember her telling me that, when I first started dating Jason," Ella says.

"You need to do what makes you happy, and not what makes everyone around you happy. Because in the end, you're the only one who has to live with your choices." Sage's mom adds.

"I remember my mom saying that to me a few times over the years." I try to force a smile. "Okay, enough about me. Someone else spill their guts."

"Well, I got word that I got my cosmetology license!" Ella says, and we all start to cheer. We were excited for her because Ella had been working at the front desk and cleaning the stations at the salon since she left school.

"Just in time for me to work part-time for a month or two, before I have the baby," she laughs. "We will make it work with whatever schedule you want," Megan says.

"There are perks to being the boss's sister-in-law," she winks.

"Maggie, are you nervous to be getting married?" Riley asks.

Maggie and Nick's nuptials are next weekend, and I'm really excited to see Greg in action. He says weddings are his favorite part of the job, being part of a new start and seeing so much love.

Other than Sage's parents, he's the one who married Sage's siblings, and the other couples here tonight. Though he didn't marry Anna Mae and Royce, since they had drunkenly got married in Las Vegas, but he did perform their vow renewal, so they had a nice memory, celebrating their marriage.

I'd love to be part of that. Helping couples start a new life, and then later help bring a new life into the world. There would be no better feeling than being there from the beginning, and then to be part of a couple's journey in starting a family.

Lots of thoughts swirl around in my head, as the night comes to an end. The non-pregnant girls have had a bit to drink, and it's loud, so I slip out onto the front porch and sit on the swing, just staring into the night.

I'm not sure how long I'm there before someone sits down next to me.

"Hiding out here?" Greg asks.

"They have been drinking, and it got to be a bit much," I shrug.

"Yeah, they can get a bit rowdy. You are coming to the budget meeting tomorrow, right?"

"Yes, I'll be there. I have all the paperwork."

He shifts, and his shoulder touches mine, and once again, I feel a spark and his warmth, and I want to get even closer to him. William's touch never feels like this. I have a lot to figure out.

"I'm going to head to bed. I'll see you tomorrow." I say, standing up.

Greg watches me and looks over my face for a moment, before standing up as well.

"See you tomorrow." He nods and heads to his truck.

I get the feeling tomorrow is going to be more than a simple carnival budget meeting with some of the other church members.

Chapter 11

Greg

A bby smiles at me and bites her lip in a way that drives me crazy. I know she's doing it on purpose. When her hand lands on my chest, just the feeling of it there, makes me hard. When she slowly drags her hand down my chest, I find it hard to breathe.

Her hand stops at my belt, and I can't stop myself anymore. I don't want to. I lean down and kiss her. The moment my lips touch hers, I'm gone. This woman owns my heart and soul.

She untucks my shirt and slides her arms around my waist under it. The skin-on-skin short circuits my brain. There's no other explanation for it.

I back her up until she's at my bed, and I lay her down. She looks like an angel, laying there looking back up at me. Then, I remove my shirt, and I watch her eyes travel up my stomach to my chest. Wasting no time, I climb onto the bed and slowly push up her dress, until her white, lace panties are visible.

They're soaked, and she's already moaning for me. Pulling her panties to the side, I quickly and eagerly take my first taste of her. I'm not disappointed. She tastes sweet and perfect. My cock is so hard from wanting her, that I have to free it. I reach down and pull it out of my pants.

The more she moans and digs her hands into my hair, the more I want to be enveloped in her heat, and the more I want her. But I need her to cum more than anything. So, as I continue to make love to her pussy with my mouth, I start humping the bed to get some relief.

"Greg, Greg, Greg." She chants, before her whole body locks up, as the orgasm washes over her.

Unable to stop myself, I cum all over the bed, just as my phone starts ringing.

My eyes pop open. These sexy dreams of Abby are getting more and more vivid. Of course, now I have to clean myself up and wash the sheets. I groan as the phone keeps ringing. Finally, without checking the caller ID, I reach over for it.

"Hello?"

"Greg." Abby sighs, and my cock is instantly hard again.

"Abby, everything okay?"

"Yes, I'm sorry to call so early. I was wondering if I should stop at the cafe and get some donuts and coffee since it's a morning meeting."

This woman is so thoughtful and perfect. Every day I spend with her, I fall a bit more. This is a dangerous ride, and unfortunately, one I'm not willing to get off any time soon.

"I actually put an order in with Jo. She will have it ready. If you would pick it up for me, that would be a huge help." When I look at the clock, I realize I'm already getting a late start.

"Okay, I'll stop and pick up the order. See you soon," she says.

As soon as she hangs up, I jump up, take a cold shower, and then toss my sheets in the wash, and then make my bed with some clean ones. Before

I get anything else done, I take Bluebell out and toss a ball with her for a few minutes to let her run off some energy, and then come in and feed her. I quickly pick up the house, and I'm just starting the dishwasher when there's a knock on the door.

I open it to find Abby there with the bags from Jo and wearing the same dress I saw in my dream. It's my favorite dress of hers, and the one she wore the first time she was at my house.

Taking the bags from her, I let her follow me back towards the kitchen, as I try to get myself under control. Bluebell greets her and buys me some time.

"Sorry, I'm a bit early. Everyone had already left the house, and I didn't want to just sit in that big house alone anymore."

"You're welcome here anytime, no notice needed." I hear myself saying it and wonder what the hell I'm thinking. It's true, but a bad idea.

The smile that covers her face makes me forget what a bad idea it is.

"How's Bluebell been doing?" She asks.

"She's spoiled. When we watch TV, she almost lies in my lap, and at night, she sleeps in bed with me. Even though she's been going almost everywhere with me in town, still no one knows her, or where she came from."

Our eyes lock again, and I open my mouth to tell her how beautiful she is, and how much I like that dress, when a knock on the door stops me, which is probably for the best.

"Mrs. Willow, come in," I say, as I open the door. She sees Abby and stops short, but doesn't say anything.

To break the awkward moment, Abby says, "I just got here. I picked up the order from Jo. Hope you're hungry."

"Child, the food is why most of us come to these meetings. Jo's donuts and coffee are just the things to start your day." She and Abby walk back towards the kitchen when there's another knock on the door. Opening it, I find Hunter's mom, Donna, Sage's mom, Helen, and Ruby Lyn.

I make a note to keep myself in check, because between Ruby Lyn and Mrs. Willow, these two are the biggest gossips in town.

We fill our plates and sit down at the dining room table. The only available seat left is either next to Abby or across from her. I take the one across from her, so I'm able to look at her and can avoid the accidental touches that might give me away.

This meeting is really an excuse to get together and chat, have some good food, and spend some time together. The money gets spent the same way every year, as forty percent goes into the community fund. This is used for helping people in need. Like when Mr. Bennett's barn burned down last year, we used it to help him rebuild.

"I think some of the community funds should be used to help Mike and Lilly with the horses they're taking in from this illegal rodeo," Ruby Lyn says.

We all agree. "We can cover Hunter's medical expenses for taking care of them since we know he won't let us pay for his time," I say, smiling at his mom.

Then, we agree to put ten percent away for next year's carnival, twenty-five percent for church operating costs, and the last twenty-five percent goes in the bank for other church events.

"Now that the business is out of the way, tell me, Abby. How is Ella doing with this pregnancy?" Ruby Lyn asks.

"She's taking it easy and is a bit tired, but otherwise good. No change, since you asked Megan earlier this week." She winks at her, and I know in that moment, I fall completely for this woman.

Abby can hold her own with these ladies. Even if I wanted to, there's no way I could stop myself from falling over that cliff. Probably, I'll hit every bump on the way down, too. So, for now, I can only hold on for the ride.

Ruby Lyn chuckles, and Mrs. Willow jumps in.

"Anna Mae is doing good as well, and my grandson, Jesse, is moving back to town next week. He finally left that cheating good for nothing wife of his. Anna Mae is thrilled to have her bother close by for the rest of the pregnancy. Until he figures out his next steps, he's going to be staying with Anna Mae and Royce."

"Wasn't he working in New York City?" I ask.

"Yeah, some money investment stuff. He says he doesn't want to live in the city anymore and wants to be here with family, so he has to figure out how to make that happen."

"Well, if we can help you, let us know," Helen says, and everyone agrees.

We talk a bit more about how Ford is doing, taking over the ranch from his folks, and how the newest rescue horse is doing. She just got released to Mike and Lilly's ranch and doesn't trust people, but is expected to survive.

The conversation moves on to Bluebell, and she soaks up everyone's attention before the ladies start leaving to get on with their day.

When it's just Abby and I left, we stare at each other for a little bit, before she stands up.

"Let me help you clean up." She begins picking up the plates off the table.

"You don't have to do that," I tell her and try to take the plates from her.

"Honestly, I'd like something to do, so I don't have to go back to the ranch just yet. I'm not used to all this free time, and I'm going a little stir crazy," she says.

"Well, I was going to take Bluebell for a walk, before I head to the church. Would you like to join us?"

"Yeah, I would." She says as we head out to walk the back of the property.

At first, we walk in silence, just watching Bluebell ahead of us.

Not sure I want to know the answer, I ask her, "Do you have a date for Nick and Maggie's wedding tomorrow?"

"No. William was going to come down for the weekend, but then, he got the chance for some extra hours helping his boss out, so he took it," she shrugs.

"Well, will you save me a dance?" My question seems to catch her off guard.

"Of course. I'm actually excited to see you perform the ceremony."

It's mutual then because I'm excited for her to be there and see it too, only I don't tell her that. I don't want to feed into this any more than I already am.

"There have been a lot of weddings in town recently. I guess they come in waves. Should be a lot of new babies in the coming years, too." I hint at her.

"Yeah, I really wish I could be here when Ella has her baby, but she's due in November, and I'll be right in the middle of clinical, so I doubt I'll be able to make it."

"Well, you don't want to miss any classes. They are important. You're going to make a great midwife. I've noticed that you're patient and caring. You naturally set people at ease, and that will be especially important, because parents will need that, especially new ones."

"Thanks, that's what my instructor said, too. Even though this is what I've wanted to do for so long, something just feels off, though. Maybe, it's just because my parents aren't here by my side through it." She says as we reach the creek.

Bluebell runs up and down beside the creek for a few minutes, before we turn to head back.

"The whole town will be at the wedding. It will be a great place to meet people and put some faces to the names you keep hearing." I tell her.

"I'm sure I've met most of them, and I just can't remember. I'm horrible with names, and at church, there are so many all at once."

"If you can't remember their name, just smile and ask how they're doing, and what's new with them. Most will be happy to talk about themselves. In most cases, that will trigger something to help you remember who they are. I did a lot of that when I first got here."

"They never caught on?" She asks.

"Nope, they were happy to talk about their kids, grandkids, parents, or whatever else was going on. They're just happy you show a bit of interest. If all else fails, stick to my side. I'll help you navigate."

"I'll take you up on that," she says, as we reach the house.

It's only once she leaves that I realize I just all but invited her to be my date by having her stick to my side at the wedding.

I can only hope I don't blow this up. In my mind, I can hear my sister yelling that I'm walking a fine line right now.

Abby smiles at me and bites her lip in a way that
drives me crazy. I know she's doing it on purpose.
When her hand lands on my
chest, just the feeling of it there, makes me hard.
When she slowly drags her hand down my chest,
I find it hard to breathe.

Her hand stops at my belt, and I can't stop
myself anymore. I don't want, too. I lean down and
kiss
her. The moment my lips touch hers, I'm gone.
This
woman owns my heart and soul.

She untucks my shirt and slides her arms around
my waist under it. The skin-on-skin short circuits
my brain. There's no other
explanation for it.

I back her up, until she's at my bed, and I lay
her down. She looks like an angel, laying there
looking back up at me. Then, I
remove my shirt, and I watch her eyes travel up
my stomach to my chest. Wasting
no time, I climb onto the bed and slowly push up
her dress, until her white,
lace panties are visible.

They're soaked, and she's already
moaning for me. Pulling her panties to the side, I
quickly and eagerly take my
first taste of her. I'm not disappointed. She tastes
sweet and perfect. My cock
is so hard from wanting her, that I have to free it.

I reach down and pull it

out of my pants.

The more she moans and digs her hands into my

hair, the more I want to be enveloped in her heat, and

the more I want her. But I need her to cum more than anything. So, as I

continue to make love to her pussy with my mouth, I start humping the bed to

get some relief.

"Greg, Greg, Greg." She chants, before

her whole body locks up, as the orgasm washes over her.

Unable to stop myself, I cum all over the bed,

just as my phone starts ringing.

My eyes pop open. These sexy dreams of Abby are

getting more and more vivid. Of course, now I have to clean myself up and wash the

sheets. I groan, as the phone keeps ringing. Finally, without checking

the caller ID, I reach over for it.

"Hello?"

"Greg." Abby sighs, and my cock is

instantly hard again.

"Abby, everything okay?"

"Yes, I'm sorry to call so early. I was

wondering if I should stop at the cafe and get some donuts and coffee, since

it's a morning meeting."

This woman is so thoughtful and perfect. Every

day I spend with her, I fall a bit more. This is a dangerous ride, and

unfortunately, one I'm not willing to get off any time soon.

"I actually put an order in with Jo. She
will have it ready. If you would pick it up for me,
that would be a
huge help." When I look at the clock, I realize I'm
already getting a late
start.
"Okay, I'll stop and pick
up the order. See you soon," she says.
As soon as she hangs up, I jump up, take a cold
shower,
and then toss my sheets in the wash, and then
make my bed with some clean ones.
Before I get anything else done, I take Bluebell out
and toss a ball with her
for a few minutes to let her run off some energy,
and then come in and feed
her. I quickly pick up the house, and I'm just
starting the dishwasher, when
there's a knock on the door.
I open it to find Abby there with the bags from
Jo and wearing the same dress I saw in my dream.
It's my favorite dress of hers,
and the one she wore the first time she was at my
house.
Taking the bags from her, I let her follow me
back towards the kitchen, as I try to get myself
under control. Bluebell greets
her and buys me some time.
"Sorry, I'm a bit early.
Everyone had already left the house, and I didn't
want
to just sit in that big house alone anymore."
"You're welcome here anytime, no notice
needed." I hear myself saying it and wonder what
the hell I'm thinking.
It's true, but a bad idea.

The smile that covers her face makes me forget what a bad idea it is.

"How's Bluebell been doing?" She asks.

"She's spoiled. When we watch TV, she almost lies in my lap, and at night, she sleeps in bed with me. Even though she's been going almost everywhere with me in town, still no one knows her, or where she came from."

Our eyes lock again, and I open my mouth to tell her how beautiful she is, and how much I like that dress, when a knock on the door stops me, which is probably for the best.

"Mrs. Willow, come in," I say, as I open the door. She sees Abby and stops short, but doesn't say anything.

To break the awkward moment, Abby says, "I just got here. I picked up the order from Jo. Hope you're hungry."

"Child, the food is why most of us come to these meetings. Jo's donuts and coffee are just the things to start your day." She and Abby walk back towards the kitchen, when there's another knock on the door. Opening it, I find Hunter's mom, Donna, Sage's mom, Helen, and Ruby Lyn.

I make a note to keep myself in check, because between Ruby Lyn and Mrs. Willow, these two are the biggest gossips in town.

We fill our plates and sit down at the dining room table. The only available seat left is either next to Abby or across from her. I take the one across from her, so I'm able to look at her and can avoid

the accidental touches that might give me away.

This meeting is really an excuse to get together

and chat, have some good food, and spend some time together. The money gets

spent the same way every year, as forty percent goes into the community fund.

This is used for helping people in need. Like when Mr. Bennett's barn burned

down last year, we used it to help him rebuild.

"I think some of the community funds should

be used to help Mike and Lilly with the horses they're taking in from this

illegal rodeo," Ruby Lyn says.

We all agree. "We can cover Hunter's medical

expenses for taking care of them, since we know he won't let us pay for his

time," I say, smiling at his mom.

Then, we agree to put ten percent away for next

year's carnival, twenty-five percent for church operating costs, and the last

twenty-five percent goes in the bank for other church events.

"Now that the business is out of the way, tell me, Abby. How is Ella doing

with this pregnancy?" Ruby Lyn asks.

"She's taking it easy and is a bit tired, but otherwise

good. No change, since you asked Megan earlier this week." She winks at

her, and I know in that moment, I fall completely for this woman.

Abby can hold her own with these ladies. Even if

I wanted to, there's no way I could stop myself from falling over that cliff.

Probably, I'll hit every bump on the way down, too. So, for now, I can only

hold on for the ride.

Ruby Lyn chuckles, and Mrs. Willow jumps in.

"Anna Mae is doing good as well, and my grandson,

Jesse, is moving back to town next week. He finally left that cheating good for

nothing wife of his. Anna Mae is thrilled to have her bother close by for the

rest of the pregnancy. Until he figures out his next steps, he's going to be

staying with Anna Mae and Royce."

"Wasn't he working in New York City?" I

ask.

"Yeah, some money investment stuff. He says

he doesn't want to live in the city anymore and wants to be here with family,

so he has to figure out how to make that happen."

"Well, if we can help you, let us know," Helen says,

and everyone agrees.

We talk a bit more about how Ford is doing,

taking over the ranch from his folks, and how the newest rescue horse is doing.

She just got released to Mike and Lilly's ranch and doesn't trust people, but is expected to

survive.

The conversation moves on to Bluebell, and she

soaks up everyone's attention, before the ladies start leaving to get on with

their day.

When it's just Abby and I left, we stare at each other for a little bit, before she stands up.

"Let me help you clean up." She begins
picking up the plates off the table.
"You don't have to do that," I tell her
and try to take the plates from her.
"Honestly, I'd like something
to do, so I don't have to
go back to the ranch just yet. I'm not used to all
this free time, and I'm
going a little stir crazy," she says.
"Well, I was going to take Bluebell for a
walk, before I head to the church. Would you like
to
join us?"
"Yeah, I would." She says, as we head out
to walk the back of the property.
At first, we walk in silence, just watching
Bluebell ahead of us.
Not sure I want to know the answer, I ask her,
"Do you have a date for Nick and Maggie's
wedding tomorrow?"
"No. William was going to come down for the
weekend, but then, he got the chance for some
extra hours helping his boss out,
so he took it," she shrugs.
"Well, will you save me a
dance?" My question seems to catch her off
guard.
"Of course. I'm actually excited to see you
perform the ceremony."
It's mutual then, because I'm excited for her to
be there and see it too, only I don't tell her that. I
don't want to feed
into this anymore than I already am.
"There have been a lot of weddings in town
recently. I guess they come in waves. Should be a

lot of new babies in the
coming years, too." I hint at her.

"Yeah, I really wish I could be here, when
Ella has her baby, but she's due in November, and I'll be right in
the middle of clinical, so I doubt I'll be able to make it."

"Well, you don't want to miss any classes. They
are important. You're going to make a great midwife. I've noticed that you're
patient and caring. You naturally set people at ease, and that will be
especially important, because parents will need that, especially new
ones."

"Thanks, that's what my instructor said, too. Even though
this is what I've wanted to do for so long, something just
feels off, though. Maybe, it's just because my parents aren't here by my side
through it." She says, as we reach the creek.
Bluebell runs up and down beside the creek for a few minutes, before we turn to head back.

"The whole town will be at the wedding. It
will be a great place to meet people and put some faces to the names you keep
hearing." I tell her.

"I'm sure I've met most of them, and I just can't
remember. I'm horrible with names, and at church, there are so many all at
once."

"If you can't remember their name, just smile and ask
how they're doing, and what's new with them. Most will be happy to talk about

themselves. In most cases, that will trigger something to help you remember

who they are. I did a lot of that, when I first got here."

"They never caught on?" She asks.

"Nope, they were happy to

talk about their kids, grandkids, parents, or whatever else

was going on. They're just happy you show a bit of interest. If all else fails, stick to my side. I'll help you navigate."

"I'll take you up on that," she says, as

we reach the house.

It's only once she leaves that I realize I just

all but invited her to be my date by having her stick to my side at the

wedding.

I can only hope I don't blow this up. In my mind,

I can hear my sister yelling that I'm walking a fine line right now.

Chapter 12

Abby

Sage, Colt, and I just got to the church for the wedding today. I can't wait to see Greg in action. He was great at making me feel at ease about not knowing everyone's names or recognizing them.

Since I don't expect to see him, before the ceremony, I'm standing outside the church-, watching people come in and chat. Today in town-, this seems to be the place to be. When I feel someone wrap an arm around my waist, I jump, turning to find Greg, smiling down at me.

"You look breathtaking in that dress." He says to me with a glint in his eye.

"Thank you. You look really good in a suit." I don't hide that I'm checking him out. That seems to only make him smile more. He grips my waist a bit tighter, before dropping his arm.

"Well, it's not every day a pretty girl I want to impress is in the audience watching me perform a wedding. I figure I should put my best foot forward." He winks at me.

This makes me blush. He's openly flirting with me. Though, I know he is, I'm not sure how to handle it, because he knows about William, but I like this side of him. Does he know about my feelings, and how my feelings for him and William are warring against each other right now? I hope not. I don't know how to put that into words, and I don't want to deal with it right now.

I'm saved from having to answer him, as people start coming up to talk, and he introduces me to everyone, just like he promised he would. Whatever conversation he's having, he pulls me into it, too. I'm a little alarmed by how good it feels to be by his side. Almost too good, and way too comfortable.

As I take my seat, waiting for the ceremony to start, I look around the church. It's an old, country church with wood plank walls painted white, lots of windows for natural light, a stained-glass window on stage, wood floors, and wooden pews.

The church may be small, but it's well maintained and well loved. It looks like something out of a magazine, or that should be at one of those open-air museums; not to be used every Sunday.

I know Greg loves being the pastor here and being the one caring for the history of the church, and the people in this town. He loves the community aspect and being able to reach out to people in town versus the big city vibe. That's when my brain goes down a dangerous path. What would it be like to be a pastor's wife here? Not just any pastor's wife, but Greg's.

It was never something I wanted to do or even considered. After my parents died, I didn't have the best experience with the leaders in my parents' church. In fact, most of them are in jail now, thanks to Sage and Colt's help.

But sitting here now, looking at Greg, I can't help but imagine being not only his wife but a pastor's wife here at this church and in this town. It really wouldn't be much different than the last few weeks, would it? Organizing this summer carnival would normally be his wife's job.

Standing by his side, and greeting people before and after church, would be his wife's job. Organizing volunteers for events would be his wife's job, too.

Where would being a midwife fit in? William has ideas of me giving that up to be a stay-at-home wife and mom. I don't want that. Would Greg expect me to give that up to be his wife? Would he expect me to take on all the church events? I want to ask, but it's extremely inappropriate, considering we aren't even dating.

I'm saved from my downward spiral, as the ceremony starts. Maggie and Nick decided to keep the wedding party small, even though they opened the wedding up to the entire town. Maggie's brother, Royce, is a groomsman, and his wife, Anna Mae, is a bridesmaid. Maggie's sister, Ella, is her Maid of Honor, and Ella's husband, Jason, is the best man since he's also Nick's best friend and business partner.

The church is packed, and there are no empty seats. People are standing in the back and along the sides. There was no way anyone was missing it. This is the place to be today. Especially, since Nick is an amazing chef, and he's testing some new recipes at the reception. This just shows how well-loved Nick and Maggie are, and how strong the town's bond really is.

As the ceremony starts, my eyes are glued not to the bride or groom, but to Greg. He stands at the front of the church, bible in hand, commanding everyone's attention. His eyes land on me every few minutes, and I think I'm imagining his smile growing when they do. While the service has classic touches in it, its personalized to Maggie and Nick, and one of the most beautiful weddings I've ever been to.

There's a mingling session, while the wedding party gets photos taken, and I scout out the appetizers and enjoy seeing everyone interact. I'm so engrossed in watching all the women come up and steal some time with Blaze and Riley's daughter that I don't notice a woman approach me.

"Are you Abby, Sage's friend?" She says in a southern Texas drawl.

"I am." I smile at her.

"I've heard your name mentioned from several of my patients. I'm Dr. Shelly, the OB Doctor. Your friend told me to reach out to you."

She is Ella, Megan, and Anna Mae's baby doctor. They have nothing but good things to say about her. I think Anna Mae is visiting her, too.

"Nice to meet you. My friends have all loved having you at their births."

"I love hearing that. Living in this area, it's wonderful to watch the babies I deliver grow up. I've heard mentioned that you are going to school to become a midwife?"

"I am. I start working with a local midwife and attending births this fall. It'll be exciting to get hands-on experience."

"Well, I know this might not be in your plans, and I know you live out of state, but my practice grew faster than I expected, and many of the families here prefer to do at home births. I've been looking to add a midwife to my office, and I'm happy to help you finish up school. You'd have a built-in job here. We service a few towns in this county and the next."

"Are you serious?" I ask, shocked.

"Very. I know I've taken you by surprise, but it's a big decision to make, where you plan to practice and put down roots, and you have connections here. Riley, Ella, Megan, and Anna Mae all speak very highly of you. I know you helped Riley, before she got to the hospital that night, too. Just think about it. You seem to have a good support system here." She hands me her card.

I take it and stare at it, still completely shocked, as everyone starts moving into the reception hall.

"Everything okay?" Greg asks as he walks up beside me.

"I feel like being here this summer is a test," I tell him.

The smile falls from his face for just a moment, before he forces it back on.

"What do you mean?"

"It's the fight against who I want to be, and who I should be. I thought coming out here and getting away from my life in Arkansas would make things clearer; let me see my choices better. It's only made it more complicated." I look into his beautiful eyes and take a deep breath.

"Sometimes, the path you're on isn't the one you're meant to stay on. So many people find God led them down a road they never expected. Don't shut Him out just because it's different." He says softly.

"What's that line from Gone with The Wind? I'll worry about it tomorrow. Today, is all about Nick and Maggie," I say, and then I pocket the business card to check out later. It can't hurt to look up her website, right?

Walking into the reception hall, I start to see a whole new life. One where I might fit in here, live here and work here. I have to shut the idea down to focus on everyone who comes up to talk to me.

Lilly makes some not-so-subtle hints at how great her husband's best friend, Ford, is, and how he just took over his family's ranch, and she could set me up on a date if I wanted. I let her down easily, telling her I was seeing someone back home.

I honestly don't think I'm the girl she has in mind for Ford. Something in the glint of her eye, as she looked at Greg when she said it, made me think she was trying to push him or find a way to get me to stay.

Ford is a nice guy don't get me wrong. He's just not the one I have my eye on, and he doesn't make me feel even one-tenth of what Greg does.

Greg was in earshot of my slow letdown to Lilly and didn't look happy at the reminder. Maybe, I need to remind us a bit more about William. So, in order to do just that, I snap a few photos and send them off to him.

Me: Maggie and Nick's wedding is packed. I think everyone in town is here tonight.

I don't get a reply right away, so I mingle a bit more and get another water.

William: You staying safe?
Me: Yes, I came with Sage and Colt, and the pastor has been introducing me to people. We have been talking up the carnival.

He must be working because his replies are slow and each ten or more minutes apart.

William: I miss you. I really wish I could have been there with you this weekend.
Me: I know, but we will get to have some fun at the carnival, so I'm looking forward to that.

Am I really looking forward to it? If I'm being honest with myself, not really. I want to experience the carnival with Greg as much as I can. But maybe having William here, will help me figure out everything going on in my head.

William: Me too. Have to go, but keep sending me pictures. I'll call you later tonight.
Me: I will. Don't work too hard.

I don't get anything back from him, as I glance around the reception hall. Couples start filling up the dance floor, and the music picks up, now that everyone seems to be done snacking on the appetizers.

When my eyes lock with Greg's, all thoughts of William are gone, and my mind has one thing on it.

To get into Greg's arms.

Chapter 13
Greg

I loved walking to the reception with Abby on my arm and almost got to pretend it was a date. But I'm still trying to make sense of what she said before we walked in, and I don't want to push her. She has a lot to figure out on her own, and as much as it kills me to stand back, I need to let her do it. As I watch, she heads off to talk to Sage and the girls all holding babies, and I go to get a drink.

Looking around, seeing her laughing and smiling, I get a glimpse of what could be of our future. Our wedding. Though, I think I'd want Ian to marry us right here in this church. The church ladies would make it over-the-top, and a wonderful celebration that the entire town would show up for.

I'm talking about it being an even bigger event than the summer carnival. Since the day I moved here, I think they have secretly been planning my wedding, and the only missing piece is the bride.

They would be just as excited as Abby and me about a wedding. It's been their goal to try to marry me off for a few years now, and each week, they always had someone new in mind for me to date. Now that I think about it, they haven't mentioned me going on a date with anyone in a few weeks.

Maybe, they ran out of candidates. I wonder if I could get that lucky. Though, I know they mean well, the break has been nice. I won't look a gift horse in the mouth. Then, a fleeting thought crosses my mind. What if they picked up on something between Abby and me, and they're planning to push their matchmaking on her?

But I don't get a chance to work myself up about it too much before people start coming over to talk to me.

"Good service," Ford says, walking up beside me.

"Thanks, I enjoy weddings. They're the highlight of the job."

If I'm honest, I don't know a pastor alive who doesn't like doing weddings and baptisms. They're the good parts of life, the happy parts. Normally, they bring the community and families together-. Then, there's always enough family drama and bloopers to make it entertaining, because nothing ever goes completely right.

"I'm guessing funerals are the downside." He says, taking a drink.

"Yeah, but knowing I can give peace to a grieving family helps. It's also another reason I enjoy the small towns. The funerals are pretty few and far between." I knock on wood to make my point.

"Who are you hiding from?" I nod out towards the crowd.

He chuckles, "Lilly. I think she has this idea about setting me up with Abby. She's been trying to fix me up with any single lady she can."

Heat races through my veins like I just slugged a shot of whiskey. I feel very protective of Abby. That's what I tell myself because I can't let what I'm feeling be jealousy or anger. She isn't mine.

"Abby is dating someone back home," I tell him.

That should be an end to any of his ideas about taking Lilly up on those suggestions.

"Ahhh, you would think Lilly knows that."

"She should. Sage and everyone at the ranch know. They have been together for a while," I say, hating the words, as they roll off my tongue.

"Well, then it's the perfect excuse when she brings it up again," he says.

"Again?"

"Yeah, Lilly already tried to get me to be Abby's date at this wedding, but she turned me down-, saying she had a date already. I guess that was you, seeing as you two walked in together." He says casually.

Not saying anything, I just let my eyes find her again in the crowd. Almost like she can sense me looking at her, she turns my way and smiles. Until it's time to eat, we're all supposed to socialize some more, so that's what I do.

When we sit down to eat, the entire time I'm watching Abby, as she talks to people at our table, laughing, and joking. Once she finishes eating, she takes Megan's baby, Willow, so Megan and Hunter can eat.

Seeing her with a baby, like it's second nature, twists my gut. She's going to be an amazing midwife and an even better mom. Whoever the guy is that gets to live that life by her side, is going to be lucky, and I hope he realizes that.

By the time Megan and Hunter are done, Abby has Willow back asleep.

"You guys go mingle and dance. I promise I've got her," Abby says to Megan.

"Oh, eating dinner peacefully was enough. You came to enjoy the wedding, not babysit," Megan says.

"Listen, it's been a while since I got some baby to cuddle. Let me snuggle her, and you go have some fun. When you come back, she will still be asleep," Abby urges.

"Come on, Meg. Let's go say hello to Anna Mae and Royce," Hunter says, placing his hands on her shoulder and steering her to the other side of the room.

I chuckle, and Abby smiles.

"It's hard for parents, especially new parents, to allow someone else to care for their kid. They feel like they have to do everything. But them relaxing a bit, will do both of them and the baby some good," Abby says. "You can go socialize. I'm good here."

"I'm right where I need to be." Is all I say, and she doesn't push the subject either.

As the dancing starts, Abby hands baby Willow back over to Megan. I lean over to whisper in her ear. Not because I need to, but because I want to be close.

"Dance with me?"

"I don't think that's a good idea." She says breathlessly.

"It's just a dance. Nothing more." I say, looking into her gorgeous eyes.

She hesitates only a moment, before nodding and letting me lead her onto the dance floor.

Wrapping my arm around her waist, and then taking her hand in mine, we start moving with the music. I make sure to keep some distance between us, as we don't need any more gossiping than there already is.

"So, I heard you had a date here tonight. What happened to him?" I ask, trying to keep my tone friendly.

"William was supposed to come down for the weekend." She says, and my whole body goes stiff. Even if tried, I don't think I could have stopped it.

"But something came up at work, and he's in line for a promotion, so I told him not to worry about me." She continues, and I relax slightly.

With that out of the way, the fact that I have her in my arms starts to take over, making my heart race. Nothing has ever felt so right.

"Well, if he was here, I wouldn't be able to have this dance with you, so in a way, I'm glad he's not."

"Hmm, I'm sure that's not the only reason you're glad he isn't here." She smirks at me, and I have to wonder if she realizes the dangerous game she's playing with me right now. This is a fine line, and we're already walking on the edge, so either one of us could go right over.

With all this talk of William, and her having a date here tonight, I'm all worked up. When her tongue flicks out to wet her perfectly plump lips, my attention is riveted on her, and I can't pull my eyes away from those lusciously soft lips.

I don't realize I'm leaning into her, until her lips part, and I can feel her warm breath on my skin. That's the moment it hits me. We're on a crowded dance floor in the middle of a wedding with the entire town surrounding us.

Thankfully, the song ends, and I step away from her, putting space between us and hating every inch between us at the same time.

She clears her throat. "Thank you for the dance."

I nod, not trusting my voice, and watch her walk over to where Sage is. When I turn to find Blaze and his brothers by the bar watching me, I head over to get a drink, something a bit stronger than water this time.

I know I'm going to have to face the music sometime, and they may not be her family, but she's Sage's friend, so that means these men will protect Abby from anyone and everyone, including the town pastor.

Colt speaks up first, "You like her."

It's a statement, not a question, but I answer anyway.

"Yeah, I do."

"But she's dating William," Mac states the obvious.

Their faces are hard, but not judging, like I'd expect they'd look. Maybe, thoughtful with a tint of sadness in them.

"I know," I sigh.

"So, what are you going to do about it?" Colt asks.

Colt is a big action person, which is funny because for many years, he didn't act on his feelings for Sage when she came back to town. He tells me they wasted many years because neither of them made that first move, and if he could do it all over again, he'd have gone after her sooner. So, I know why he's asking.

"I wish I knew. She's dating someone else, and I refuse to be the guy that breaks them up, but the more I'm around her, the more of a chance there is I'm going to slip up. I don't trust myself."

"I know the feeling," Jason says.

I glance back over to her where she's lost in conversation and smiling, and I know I'd give anything for her to be mine. But there are just some lines I can't cross, as the town's pastor, and giving up my spot, as the town pastor, just isn't an option.

Chapter 14

Abby

You know that moment when you stare at a word long enough, and the way it's spelled you aren't sure if it's correct anymore? That's how it feels looking at the words 'pie auction.' And just the word pie in general.

Setting up for the pie contest, auction, and sale today has been something else. Everyone in town has opinions, and as much as they mean well, it just makes something that should have only taken the morning to do last all day.

The plan has changed at least four different times. The setup of tables keeps moving, and most of the time, I don't even get a heads up. I'm not sure why they need someone in charge of it all, because they just override me. But in the end, it looks great, even if it's finally set up the way we had it planned in the beginning.

"Abby, can you help me with the rope on the last tent?" Ford asks.

Setting my clipboard down, I hold the rope where he asks me, while he and a few other guys get the tent in place. Instead of paying attention, I'm concentrating more on what still needs to get done and running down the list in my head. So, when the gust of wind hits my face, I don't see the corner of the tent get ripped from one of the guy's hands and whip around at me.

A searing pain radiates up my arm, before strong arms wrap around my waist, pulling me out of the way, and then setting me on a picnic bench under a nearby tent.

"Greg," I sigh, watching him checking me over.

The concern on his face makes my heart race. When was the last time someone was this worried about me? Heck, I twisted my ankle, and William barely gave me the once over, before asking if I could walk.

"You're bleeding. Wait here." He runs to his truck and comes back with a small towel that he wraps around my arm.

"Other than your arm, are you okay?" His eyes roam over my body several times.

"I think so," I say, as the other guys come running up.

"I'm so sorry, Abby. I should have had a better hold on it." The guy who was trying to secure the corner says.

I met him for the first time today. He's one of the church ladies husbands, and I can't remember his name.

"It's not your fault, because that wind came from nowhere," I say.

He doesn't look convinced, and I know he feels guilty, but there was no way to know we'd get a sudden gust of wind when we haven't had a breeze at all today.

"Let's get you to the clinic, have the doctor check you over, and clean up that cut," Greg says.

I just nod, as he wraps his arm around my waist, guiding me to his truck. Though I can walk just fine, I want his comfort more than anything right now. So, I don't push him away, like I know I should.

On the drive to the clinic, I check my phone to see if there's anything from William. He's been hard to get a hold of the last few days. I know I should let him know about my injury, but decide to wait until I hear what the doctor has to say. If he's busy at work, I don't want to worry him, especially if it's nothing, which I'm pretty sure it is.

After parking, Greg gets out and helps me from the truck. We walk inside with his arm around my waist, as he did on the way to his car.

"Hey, Pastor. Is everything okay?" A man about Sage's age comes out, wearing a doctor's coat.

"Brice, we were setting up the tents for the pie sale and a gust of wind came in. The corner of one tent got loose and sliced Abby's arm here." Greg says a bit rushed, but his voice is still steady. I finally take a good look at him, and he seems a little worried, maybe even panicked.

I place my hand on his arm. "I'm fine. It's just blood." I try to brush it off, but Greg shoots me a look like he wants to tell me it's much worse than that.

"Come back with me, and let's take a look at it," Brice says.

We follow him to one of the exam rooms, and while Brice washes his hands and puts on gloves, Greg places his hands around my waist and gently helps me up onto the table. With Greg's hands on me, I'm certainly not thinking about the cut on my arm.

I'm thinking about how I once again feel so safe in his arms, and how gentle he is. I'm thinking about being wrapped in those arms, while we cuddle on the couch, watching TV, or cuddling in bed, after a long day.

Forgetting where I am, and why I'm here, all I see is Greg. I can see a whole future ahead of us. Lazy days taking Bluebell for a walk, coming back to a home cooked meal after school or a long delivery, or being the one cooking for him, when he gets home after a long day.

"Okay, let me see that arm," Brice says, pulling me from my safe daydream bubble.

I hold up my arm that has a towel wrapped around it. He unties the towel and gently cleans up the blood to take a look at the scratch.

"It's not going to need stitches. I can close this with a dissolvable Band-Aid after I clean it up. But you'll need to give this arm a rest for the next few days. If it tears open again, it can get infected," he says.

I just nod and let him get to work cleaning it up. The area around the cut is tender, and when he hits a particularly sore spot, I grimace. Greg takes my free hand in his, and then gently turns me to face him.

No words are spoken, but the look between us says it all. That look says he's right there by my side and not going anywhere. As much as he hates to see me hurt, he's going to be my rock. I know it in my soul. That sense of safety and belonging returns, making everything more confusing, but I refuse to think about it right now.

When Brice is finished, we head out front, and I try to pay the woman at the front desk.

"No, ma'am, we have an open account with the church, and the bill will go there," she says.

"Oh, no. I don't work there. I'll pay for it." I try to correct her.

Greg steps up beside me and gently places his hand on my back, making me momentarily forget what we were talking about.

"Abby, you were working at a church event. These things happen, and it's why we have an open account with them. All volunteers are covered, so don't worry about it. If you want to pay for it, I'm sure Brice would prefer one of your pies over your money, anyway," Greg says.

"Ain't that the truth?" The lady at the front desk says with a smile.

I smile and nod, as we go out. But instead of rushing back to finish helping with the set-up, Greg takes me back to his place.

Before I can even ask why he beats me to it like he can read my mind. "The doc said you need to rest the arm, so we're going to get a report from Mrs. Willow on how the rest of set-up went and make a game plan from there. Then, you'll delegate what needs to be done." He gives me a pointed look.

I smirk at him and let him help me out of his truck and inside to the couch. He's treating me like I just had major surgery, not like I have a simple cut on my non-dominant arm. It is nice to be fussed over, even if it's completely unnecessary.

Once I'm sitting on the couch, he disappears down the hall and comes back with a pillow and a blanket. He uses the pillow to prop up my arm and sets the blanket down beside me. It's a bit much, but I do like him taking care of me. Since my parents passed, I haven't had anyone take care of me like this.

Realizing I need to text William, I reach for my phone.

"Whoa, what do you need? I can get it for you." Greg stops me.

"My phone from my purse, please." He gets it and hands it to me.

"Are you hungry? Thirsty?" He asks.

"Both. I didn't get a chance to eat lunch." I say, realizing it's already after two in the afternoon.

"Leftover baked mac and cheese, okay?"

"Perfect." He goes into the kitchen to warm up the food, and I text William to let him know about my arm, and what the doctor said. I wait and watch, but he doesn't reply.

I guess, he's even busier at work than I thought. I never gave it much thought to how much his bosses make them work, but I've heard their wives talk about how they're never home. Though they never seem to care, because they have all this money to spend, but I don't think I'd be okay with my husband not being home.

Heck, I know I wouldn't be okay getting hurt and not hearing anything from my husband like this. If I'm honest, as over the top as Greg has been at taking care of me, that's how I would expect my husband to be, when I'm hurt, because I know that's how I'd be with him.

So, when Greg brings my food and some water in, I set my phone down and give him my attention. He's here, he cares, and I know he's been worried. Giving him my attention may calm his nerves a bit.

"Thank you for all this," I say, as I dig into the food.

"Of course. To be honest, I never felt as helpless as watching Brice take care of you, and only being able to hold your hand, so I'm happy to be able to do something now."

I don't know what to say, but what I want to say isn't appropriate right now. Things like holding my hand were what I needed, and how much I needed him there. How just him holding my hand relaxed me, and how much I want him to touch me again. Instead, I change the subject.

"So, are you ready to judge the pie contest tomorrow?" I ask.

"That I'm ready for. It's hosting the auction, that I'm not so sure about."

Greg got roped into being the pie auctioneer. The church didn't want to hire someone to speak and not be able to understand them, so they picked Greg to run the auction. I don't tell him I'm looking forward to watching him.

"You'll do great," I assure him with a smile.

Chapter 15

Greg

The pie contest judging starts in an hour, and I've been running around doing all the things Abby says need to be done, so she can sit down and rest. Things like making sure everyone is set up where they should be, and everyone has signed in. Making sure tents are extra secure.

I've caught her twice trying to do things herself, so now, I've got Sage watching over her, and Colt watching over Sage. They're mostly giving directions to people who are visiting and want to check out the pies before the judging starts.

While Abby and I are both selling pies at the auction and at the sale, and since we're judging, we didn't enter them in the pie contest, which gives us a break, before the judging starts.

I grab her a bottle of water and head over to where she's sitting.

"Great, now that you're back, Colt and I are going to go grab some food, before the auction starts," Sage says and pulls Colt down the road to the diner.

He goes willingly with his arm wrapped around her holding her close, protecting her, and showing the world she's his. I want that even more now that I know I want that with is Abby. Not that I can even tell anyone about it, especially not while she's still with William.

"Drink up," I tell Abby, as I hand her the water.

"Thank you." She takes it and drinks a fourth of it, before setting it down.

"Everything ready for the judging?" She asks.

"Yep, everyone is setting up now. We have a little time before we have to meet up with the other judges. How's your arm?" I nod towards her arm that she has wrapped up to avoid anything messing with the bandage Brice put on yesterday.

"It's still a little sore to the touch, but otherwise, I forget it's there." She says, but something flashes in her eyes that I can't read.

"Everything okay?"

She sighs. "You're probably the last person I should be talking about this to, but I told William about the injury. Well I texted him, and I still haven't heard from him. I thought he'd call last night to at least see if I'm okay."

Part of me wants to track this guy down and find out what the hell his problem is. He has this great girl, and he's treating her like this? He should be worshiping the ground she walks on. The other part of me is happy he's showing his true colors, and I hope it's pushing her more and more towards Rock Springs and towards me.

"Yeah, but how many times have Sage and her family asked you?" I smile, trying to lighten the mood.

"At least twice each," she says.

"See, so that's what twenty times? I'm sure you're sick of it by now."

"Yeah, still."

"I know. But hey, at least we get to have some of the best pies this side of Dallas here in a bit."

"True. That will take your mind off anything." She jokes, and then hands me a pack of beef jerky.

"What's this?" I ask, taking it from her.

"We're getting ready to eat a lot of sugar. You need to counteract it with a bit of protein. Trust me, you'll thank me later." She nods, taking a bite of her own.

Trusting her, I take a few bites of the piece she gave me.

"So, listen. My sister, her husband, and their kids always come to town for the summer carnival. They will get in tonight, and I was wondering if you'd like to join us for dinner tomorrow?" I say hesitantly.

She has no reason to accept. We aren't a couple, and this is something you do with someone you're dating; not just friends with. She looks a bit hesitant to answer, rightfully so.

I hope she says yes, as I really want my sister to meet her. Because if I have it my way, by this time next year, she will be mine, and I want my sister to know her more than just a name.

If she's even thinking about a future with me, one-tenth as much as I do with her, then I want her to know my family. Heck, if she bonds with my sister, it might work in my favor. It could also backfire, but that's a risk I'm willing to take.

"No pressure. It's just I've been talking about you helping plan this a lot, and my sister wants to meet you. You can totally say no and just meet her at the carnival, but be warned, she won't leave town without meeting you. When she sets her mind to something, she makes it happen, or her husband will."

I'm not even close to exaggerating. That man will move heaven and earth for my sister. He's a great role model of the husband I hope to be someday.

"I guess I can do dinner tomorrow, as long as I can bring some food," she says.

"How about the dessert?" I ask.

She thinks for a moment, and then smiles, and I know I'd move heaven and hell to get her to smile at me like that again. That's how my brother-in-law describes the need to keep my sister happy. And that's how I know Abby is it for me.

"Do they have any allergies or special diets?"

"Nope, though their youngest hates blueberries."

"Not a problem." She waves her hand at me and then checks her phone. "We should go meet up with the other judges." She says, standing up.

I follow her over to where the other judges are meeting up. Joining us as judges, are Jo, the diner owner, Nick, who is the award-winning chef from WJ's bar and grill here in town, and Maria, who is Maggie and Ella's mother. Maggie ran a few of these pie contests back at her church in Tennessee before the family moved here.

Once everyone is there, Abby takes charge. I can't take my eyes off her, and I know she'll make a great pastor's wife. Heck, a great wife in general.

"Okay, the rules are simple. We're grading taste, appearance, and originality. You enter your score of one to ten on your tablet there. One being horrible, five being average, and ten being blow your mind amazing. The program will calculate a winner for us."

"Easy enough," I say, and everyone agrees. "Ready?" I lead the way down the line of pies.

There's everything from traditional apple pies to shoofly pies, Mrs. Willow's Texas bourbon pie, and some new twists on some classics.

Everyone is excited to talk about their recipe, most having been handed down for generations.

"This is why I skipped lunch," Abby says, as I taste the last pie. "I'm so full now."

"Yeah, I didn't think we'd have almost thirty entries. That was a lot of pie," I agree.

"I should have listened to Maggie and skipped lunch." Nick groans, as he holds his stomach.

We all laugh, as Abby hands him some Tums. This woman seems prepared for anything.

"All I heard was that my wife is right, and I was wrong, again," Maggie says, smiling at him and bringing him some water.

"So, who is the winner?" Maggie asks as I pull up the results. After telling them, I go to the podium to make the announcement.

"There were a lot of really good pies here today, but only one winner, and it was a clear winner, according to the program all of you church ladies made us use." I pause, and they laugh.

"The winner is... Mrs. Willow!" I say as she comes up to get her ribbon.

"Damn right! You can't go wrong with bourbon!" She says.

We give out second and third place, along with some best in categories as well.

"Now, you have an hour to window shop-, before the charity auction. The auction prices will determine the prices of the remaining pies, all of which will go to the church town relief fund."

Then, there's a flurry of activity, as everyone heads off to take a look at the pies that will be up for sale.

"The auction should be fun. I see quite a few out of towner's here." I tell Abby, as we go get some more water. On a hot, Texas summer day like today, you can't have enough water.

"Think we can get our stomachs pumped before it starts?" She groans,- as we sit down.

No sooner does my butt hit the bench, when her phone rings. She checks it, frowns, hits ignore, and puts it back in her pocket.

"Everything okay?" I ask.

"William is finally calling me back, but not like I'll be able to hear him over all this." She waves her hand at the crowd, but I can tell she's upset.

It's been almost a full twenty-four hours since she hurt herself, and he's just now getting back to her? If it was a true emergency, she could have been dead or dying. But I don't let my mind go there, as I need to stay focused on the auction ahead.

"Want me to find Sage, so you can talk to her?" I ask, thinking Sage would know what to say.

"I don't want to talk about it at all." She says, taking a deep breath. "Let's get you ready for the auction."

To say I wasn't ready for the auction, was an understatement. It was so fast-paced, and people got a bit out of hand, as we auctioned off some of the winning pies. Mrs. Willow's alone went for over one hundred dollars to some fancy type from Dallas.

Even in the chaos, there were plenty of laughs, and I will say I couldn't imagine the day without Abby having been here.

Chapter 16

Abby

Tonight, I have dinner with Greg and his sister's family. Saying I'm nervous is a bit of an understatement. We're friends, but this feels like something more. I do want to be there, but I don't want to lead anyone on either. So, I pick a somewhat casual, very modest dress and go for the girl next door look; not a 'this is a date' look.

At least, that's what Megan called it, as she did my hair for me, and Ella helped with putting on makeup that looks like I'm not wearing makeup.

Straightening my dress, I balance the dessert in one hand and knock on Greg's door with the other. Right away, he answers with a huge smile on his handsome face.

"You look beautiful." He says softly, before stepping to the side, so I can walk in. Behind him is a couple, who I assume are his sister, brother-in-law, and their kids sitting on the couch.

"This is my sister, Lizzie, and her husband, Collin. Guys, this is Abby." He introduces me to the woman who has the same dark brown hair like him, and the same beautiful coppery eyes.

The man standing next to her has blonde hair-, and if it wasn't for the wranglers, belt buckle, and button-down shirt, I'd almost assume he was a surfer with his tan skin, crooked smile, and light blonde hair.

"It's so nice to finally meet you," Lizzie says, as she pulls me in for a hug.

"Greg has a lot of great things to say about you," her husband says, as he shakes my hand.

"These are our kids, Banner and Jessa," his sister says.

"I brought Orange Crush Cupcakes for dessert. They're Riley's specialty, and she made them last time I was here, and I've wanted them ever since, so she taught me how to make them today." I ramble on, as I hand Greg the platter of cupcakes.

"They look delicious." He says, taking them back to the kitchen.

Lizzie and Collin sit on the couch with their kids, so I sit in the armchair next to the couch, and when Greg comes in, he sits in the matching armchair across from me.

"How's your arm?" Greg asks. "We had a mishap with a gust of wind catching a tent corner, and it sliced her arm," Greg tells his sister.

"Oh, it's fine; not really even sore anymore. Brice was at the house talking to Sage's dad and took a look at it. He says it's healing faster than he expected," I tell him.

"Brice is the town's doctor. He and his dad run the practice in town," Greg says.

"So, how did the pie contest and auction go?" Lizzie asks.

"It went well. The final total from the auction was just over one thousand dollars for the town relief fund, so I'm really excited," I say.

That's when Jessa walks over to me and tugs on my sleeve.

"You're very pretty. Is your hair natural, because it's the same color as my friend Jamie's mom's, but hers is from a box."? She asks me with a completely straight face.

Both Lizzie and Collin's eyes go as wide as saucers, and Greg's mouth drops open, and I can't help but laugh.

"Mine is natural. I got it from my mom, but there's nothing wrong with getting hair color from a box either. Some actors color their hair to play a part. Moms do it to give them self-confidence. Sometimes, it's just fun." I tell her.

She looks lost in thought for a moment, and then turns to her mom, "I think I'd like my hair to be pink when I'm older." Then, she walks back over to her brother, like nothing happened.

By then, all of us adults are laughing.

"I'm sorry. She's at the age, where she says what's on her mind," Collin says.

"May she never lose that, because it's a great quality," I tell him.

Turning to Greg, I ask, "Where is Bluebell?"

"In my room, the kids were playing with her earlier and tired her out, so she wants to rest," he says.

"Can I go see her? I miss her."

His sister is watching me, but I can't read her face. I don't know if it's a good thing or a bad thing. Maybe, it's the fact that I just asked to go into her brother's bedroom?

"Yeah, come on." He nods his head, and I follow him to his room and find Bluebell passed out on his bed.

Almost like she hears us come into the room, she opens her eyes. When she sees me, she lifts her head, and I sit down on the edge of the bed to pet her.

"Sorry again about Jessa." He says, sitting down to pet Bluebell as well.

"I promise, it's okay. I used to help with the kid's Sunday school at my parents' church. The kids came in asking questions only parents should answer," I laugh.

He studies me with a smile on his face, and I wish I knew what he was thinking, but I'm too scared to ask. I don't want his sister to overhear it, either.

"We should get back out there," I say barely above a whisper, and a bit of sadness is reflected in his eyes.

We head back into the living room, and he goes to the kitchen to check on dinner. I don't even get a chance to sit down before he calls that dinner is ready, and we all file into the dining room.

Once settled and grace is said, we dig in.

"I'm sorry, but I'm calling you on this. Mrs. Willow cooked dinner," I say.

"And I warmed it up," he smirks. "I can cook on a grill and heat food up. The church ladies make sure I'm fed otherwise."

Conversation over dinner flows pretty easily, and I catch Greg looking at me several times, and his sister seems to study him. We talk about Collins's job, and how the kids are doing in school. Then, we tell them the story of Bluebell, and they ask about my schooling.

After dinner, Lizzie and I do dishes, while the guys take the kids and Bluebell out to run off their energy. We're able to watch them through the kitchen window, and Greg looks so happy with his niece and nephew.

"He really likes you." She says, pulling me from my thoughts and forcing me to concentrate on her, and not the view out the window.

I don't know what to say, so I give her a small smile and turn to find her studying me.

"Greg and I talk a lot. We were really close growing up, and he's now my best friend. I know your story, about your parents, which I'm sorry about. I can't imagine losing your only family so young."

"This is where I'm supposed to say thanks, but really, I don't know what to say here. I was a robot at the funeral, and since then, it's like people are scared to talk about it." I say honestly.

"But Greg has made you think all about it? About your family, and where you want your life to go now?"

"He's made me think about it, even if he doesn't force me to talk about it too much."

"But the biggest thing is that you don't live here," she says.

"I want to, but I let people kind of take the reins after my parents died, and now, I feel trapped." I slap my hand over my mouth. "Please, forget I said that."

Where that came from, I don't know. I hadn't even admitted it to myself. The thought never crossed my mind, but somehow, it just came right out to the perfect stranger I met today.

"First time you admitted it to yourself, I'm guessing. My family and Collin say I have that effect on people. It's my super power, this ability to force people to admit to themselves what they haven't been able to before."

"Poor Collin." I smile, and she does, too.

"He's used to it by now, maybe even immune. The kids not so much. I think it's why Jess speaks her mind so well."

We both turn to watch the kids out of the window, and Greg notices us watching and gives us both a smile.

"What I'm trying to say is I've never seen him this happy. The way he looks at you, and the way you look at him, it's more than friends. It's the way Collin looks at me, and the way our parents look at each other. With your boyfriend in the picture, you need to figure out what you want, sooner rather than later, before Greg falls even more. I don't want to see him hurt."

Falls even more? He hasn't fallen for me. Sure, there are some feelings there that we haven't explored, but it's nothing past friendship. No one is falling for the other. Right?

"From the look on your face, I'm guessing you didn't realize how deep his feelings for you are, or again, you hadn't admitted it to yourself. I really like you, and I know he loves having you around, but I have to protect my brother."

"I get that. Trust me, I do." I whisper as we finish up the dishes.

My mind is anywhere but here. I don't want to hurt Greg, but I did make a commitment to this summer carnival, and I'll finish out my commitment, but maybe, it's better I head home a bit sooner than I had planned.

"Will you tell Greg I had a great time, and I'll see him at the carnival this weekend? I need to go." I set the towel I was drying dishes with down and quickly move to grab my purse.

"Abby, I didn't mean to upset you." She says, trying to come after me, but I'm already at the front door.

"You didn't. I just need to go. It was nice to meet you, and your kids are adorable. Thank you for tonight." I walk out of the door and close it behind me without looking back.

I hurry to my truck, getting inside and starting it. Only then, do I glance back behind me once I'm heading out to see Greg, rounding the corner of the house and staring after me.

The look on his face breaks my heart, but it's better this way. He will realize that soon enough.

Chapter 17

Greg

Going to bed has become one of my favorite things to do because I know, when I go to sleep, I'll see Abby. I've been dreaming of her every night. Not just sexy dreams, but normal everyday things, like being able to take her on a date, a simple kiss, her playing with Bluebell, and my favorite, her living here in Rock Springs.

Last night, I dreamed that we were at the ranch having dinner with Sage and family, and I was there as her boyfriend. We were all laughing and talking around the dinner table, and I had my arm around her waist, holding her close to me. It was perfect, until I woke up to Bluebell, licking my face.

I hate when I'm woken up from these dreams, and it takes me a minute to realize it's my phone waking me up this morning.

"Hank?" I answer, after checking the caller ID. What is Hunter's dad calling me for?

"Greg, another horse showed up in town. This time at the vet's office and my motion sensors were triggered. I thought you'd like to know since you helped with the sting. Hunter, Sage, Colt, Mike, and Lilly are on their way already."

"Thank you for calling. I'm on my way as well," I say, already getting out of bed.

It's the middle of summer, so I keep on the sweatpants, put on a shirt and my shoes, grab my phone, and wallet. Writing a quick note for my sister, I leave it on the kitchen counter and head out. When I get out of the car, I remember how Bluebell helped with the last one, so I turn around and open the door.

"Come on, girl. We're going for a ride," I say, as she comes running out and jumps right in my truck, no hesitation.

I drive towards the vet clinic, and it only takes me a few minutes to get there, since it's barely sunrise. The roads are still mostly empty. That is until I get to the vet's where there are trucks, cops, horse trailers, and other cars. I park out of the way and put on Bluebell's leash, before getting her out to follow me.

As I walk up, Colt comes over.

"Well, the mystery gets deeper. This one isn't in as bad of a shape as the others. If it weren't for some matching scars, you'd never think it was part of the same operation."

"It's almost like they're toying with us. We caught one of their guys, and now, they want to play a game." I say more to myself.

"Exactly. This one is doing so well that Hunter says it can go right to Mike and Lilly's, so they're trying to load it up now," Colt says.

"Having trouble getting it in the trailer like the last one?" I ask.

"Yep, want to let Bluebell do her thing?" He smirks.

I walk up, and as soon as I get in front of the small crowd, Hunter sees me and waves me forward.

"Think Bluebell can give us a hand?" He asks.

I unleash her, and she slowly walks up to the horse. They sniff each other and seem to have a silent conversation before Bluebell leads the horse into the trailer. Simple as that. If I didn't see it with my own eyes, I might not believe it.

"Take the horse to Mike and Lilly's. The girls are there getting a stall ready for him now. I'll stay here with the cops." Hank says as the crowd starts to leave.

"We were really hoping this would end, after the sting you helped with, but it got us nothing," Miles says.

He's one of the state troopers that have been assigned to the area, while all this is going on. He's young like me, but a bit hesitant on dating, after his run in with Maggie.

Before Maggie and Nick started dating, he tried to ask Maggie out, and Nick went off on him. Everyone thinks Miles was the final push for Nick to admit his feelings for Maggie.

So, I can't blame Miles for being hesitant to ask someone out again. It's a small town, and with his reason for being here, it's best not to make any enemies.

"Yeah, here's to praying we get a break soon. I don't know how many more horses will go missing, before the town takes it into their own hands, and then there's nothing you or I'll be able to do to stop them," I say.

"Let's hope it doesn't come to that." Even though we both know, we're there at that point.

I follow the crowd over to Mike and Lilly's ranch, which is next door to Hank's, well, as next door as a ranch can be. As everyone pulls up to the barn, Lilly, Abby, and Riley come out to greet us.

Abby is in pajama pants, boots, a t-shirt, and her hair up in a messy bun with not a stitch of makeup on. I've never seen her more beautiful. It's the first time I've seen her in pants, except for the time after Bluebell's bath. Otherwise, she's always in skirts or dresses. When she spots me, she gives me a tired smile and walks over.

"One heck of a way to be woken up, huh?" She says.

"You aren't kidding. Want to go for a walk? I have a feeling Hunter's mom will have some coffee going. We can bring some back for everyone."

"Sounds good to me." She says as we start towards the footpath that will take us to Hunter's parents' house with Bluebell in tow, excited to explore.

"Lilly was saying they just finished up the bunkhouses. They're going to give us a tour, once things settle down," Abby says.

Mike and Lilly have plans for starting a summer camp and using the horses they have been able to rehabilitate for working with the kids.

"They also said they're set up to do a short weeklong camp at the end of the month, as a trial run. They're really excited," Abby says.

"I heard about that. They're bringing in local kids, and some from Dallas, too."

We walk in silence for a moment, and once we're far enough from the barn, where no one will see us and still far enough from Hunter's parents, I stop and turn towards her.

"You okay?" I ask. I can't put my finger on it, but something seems off.

"I'm fine." She says, not looking at me. I know from experience with my sister that fine doesn't mean fine.

I reach out and gently put my hand on her arm, drawing her attention towards me.

"You can talk to me about anything you know," I tell her gently.

"It's stupid boy problems." She waves me off and starts walking again.

"Abby..."

She stops short and looks at me.

"William isn't coming down for the carnival I worked so hard on. When I told him about my arm, he didn't even ask if I was okay, and we've talked a whopping once in three days. Yet, when I got here, he was calling several times a day. I'm irritated, and I don't know how to feel about it all. I'm not a morning person, and I want coffee, so can we not do this and get coffee, please."

"Okay." I nod, taking in everything she said.

I want to tell her long distance is hard, especially when someone is working towards a promotion, as she told me William is. I want to say that, when you're apart this long, you make new routines. That maybe she should try something new. I want to tell her perhaps she's starting to see his true feelings, but I don't say any of it.

I keep my mouth shut and do the best thing I can. I take her to get coffee.

Just as I predicted, Donna has coffee going and fresh muffins coming out of the oven.

"Oh, perfect timing. You can help me carry all this back down to the barn." She greets us.

"We need to get some coffee in this one first." I joke with her, which earns me a glare and a fake smile, as Abby pours coffee, and then drinks it black.

Donna chuckles, "Early mornings like this are always hard on everyone."

"Well, I bet in all your years, as the vet's wife, you never had many mornings like this." I joke.

"Oh, I've had some bad ones. Woke up one morning to someone having left a monkey in a cage on our front porch, and he wasn't happy. Many times, I'd almost trip over boxes of puppies or kittens that people leave on our doorstep, and those buggers are worse than a newborn baby." She shakes her head, as she packs up the muffins.

"Now, come on. Let's feed everyone." She hands Abby and I both large vats of coffee and a basket of muffins to carry, before picking up her own.

"I should have brought the truck over," I grumble.

As we walk back towards the barn, Donna and Abby talk about the horses, and then the carnival that we're doing the final set up on tomorrow.

When we get there, Colt puts down his truck bed, and we set up everything. Then, everyone comes to grab food and coffee.

"Want to see the bunkhouse?" Lilly asks Abby and me.

"Yeah, let's go." I top off my coffee and finish my muffin.

We follow her to the other side of the barn to what was one of the old ranch hand bunks that they remodeled.

I've never been to summer camp, but it's pretty much as I was expecting. A large room with bunk beds lining the wall, several bathrooms, and a bed at either end for the camp counselor. There's also a seating area in the middle.

It's decorated with some of Royce's woodwork décor, and a very rustic, Texas cowboy theme.

"This is the boy's bunk. The girl's bunk is the same, just a bit pinker and with some lace," she says.

"Wow," Abby says. "This is such a night and day difference."

"We're now renovating the main house, and that seems to be more trouble. We agreed on everything out here and for the barn, but not so much on the house renovations," Lilly chuckles.

"It's more personal there," I say.

"That's true."

"Let's go check on the horses," Lilly says, as she sees the cops start to file out.

• • • • • • • • • • •

It's been a long day, but most of the carnival is set up. The company that handles the rides and games got in last night, and they're pretty much all put together and ready for the carnival. Nick is overseeing all the food trucks and stands, and they're ready to go. Jason and my sister are setting up the stage and dance floor for the bands.

Abby and I are finishing up the 4H displays and the arts and crafts booths, and then we're done for the day. I have been watching her, making sure she isn't doing anything to injure her arm again.

The problem is, the more I watch her, the more I fall for her. I realized this morning that without a doubt, I am in love with her. I think my sister saw it, before I did, but I just admitted it to myself, anyway. I'm falling hard for this woman, and she isn't even mine.

If she was mine right now, I'd walk up behind her and wrap my arms around her waist, and then pull her into me, so she can feel how hard I am. How that long maxi dress is teasing me, when the wind blows, and it molds to her curves. If she was mine, I'd be whispering all the things I plan to do to her later tonight, when we get home. If she was mine,

I'd kiss her right now in front of everyone. But she isn't mine, and I have to keep my hands and my lips to myself.

My sister walks up to me and nudges me with her shoulder.

"This looks even better than last year."

"Yeah, it does with the changes we made. We took over part of the parking for the stage and dance floor, so the high school is letting people park there after six p.m. If we expand again next year, we'll need to do something about parking." I spout off.

"Well, you have a year to work it out. I know you'll come up with something," she says.

I just nod, because I'm not able to take my eyes off of Abby. She's directing people where to go and has a smile for everyone.

When she turns to face me, we have a moment-, where our eyes meet. In that brief moment, so much more passes between us, but neither of us acts on it.

The spell is broken, when Ford walks up.

"Perfect timing. Greg, will you and Ford unload the rest of the tables for the arts and crafts booths?" Abby asks.

"Of course." I smile and head towards the box truck that delivered all the rentals.

"You got it bad, man. You aren't even trying to hide it," Ford says.

"No idea what you're talking about." I try to play it off.

"Okay, but I wasn't the only one noticing," he says, and then thankfully drops the subject.

No sooner do we unload the last table, than Mrs. Willow walks up to me.

"Have a moment to spare to show me around?" She says.

"Of course." I hold out my arm, and we start walking. But I should have known it was a trap.

"I see the way you have been watching Abby today."

"You don't know what you're seeing," I say, not meeting her eyes.

"I'm old. Not blind or senile, boy!"

I laugh at that.

"Listen, Abby would be a great wife for you. I'm willing to do what I can to help you out, but I need to know this is what you want because there are a few big hurdles in the way." She says, patting my arm.

"For one, she doesn't live here, and she has a boyfriend?" I ask.

"Among other things. Those can easily be fixed by planting the right seeds in her head."

"Plant away, Mrs. Willow. I won't turn down any help at this point. Though, I doubt it will do any good."

"Coming from you, it would do about as good as a tit on a bull. Coming from an old woman, who lived her life, it will be useful. Just trust me on this." She says with an evil smile.

"Famous last words, Mrs. Willow."

Chapter 18

Abby

Today, is the first day of the carnival being open, and I'm here with Sage and Colt.

"I can't believe how many people are here for such a small-town," I say, taking in the crowds, and how busy it is.

"People come from all over, even as far as Dallas, for the events we put on. Last year, we had some people from Houston. More so now, that Nick and WJ's is famous for their food. We have worked hard to preserve our iconic Main Street, and you can see why all the hype when you see the view from the top of The Ferris Wheel. Promise me you'll take a ride on it before the night is over," Sage says.

"I'll make sure she does," Greg says before I get a chance to answer. "How about you let me show you around, and we let Sage and Colt here have some time alone together?" He smiles and winks at the couple.

I look over at Sage, who gives me the 'only if you want to' look.

"That sounds good, so long as we can start with the food. I'm starving." I smile at him.

"Right this way." He holds out his hand towards the left of us that will lead to the food area and seating.

As I follow him, the closer we get, the more intoxicating the smells become. A few stand out, like the taco truck and the BBQ booth.

"What are you in the mood for?" He asks.

"Anything Nick made. For dessert, the grilled donut hole kabobs I saw in the booth we just passed," I say.

"Okay, why don't you grab us that picnic table over there, and I'll grab the food." He says.

I pull out some money to pay for my share.

"No way. This is my treat, as a thank you for helping with all of this."

I hesitate for a moment because it makes it feel like a date, but he said it's a thank you, so I hesitantly put my money back in my purse.

"Okay, thank you." I go and grab the table, while he gets the food.

"Hey, girl! Megs was right. You rocked this carnival." Anna Mae says as she walks up with her husband, Royce.

"Thanks, but shouldn't you be at home relaxing?"

"Are you kidding? This is all everyone at the salon has been talking about, and the pregnancy cravings are wanting funnel cakes and all things deep fried." She says, rubbing her baby belly that's just starting to show.

Anna Mae works at Megan's hair salon, and her husband, Royce, is Ella and Maggie's brother, and since their husbands, Jason and Nick, have been involved in the cooking, I'm sure she's heard even more about it.

"I'm here to make sure she doesn't attempt any rides. Food and crafts are all she promised." Royce says, wrapping an arm around her waist and looking at her like she hung the moon just for him.

Those two might have had a rocky start waking up married in Vegas, but they're so in love now; anyone can see it.

They leave just as Greg walks up with our food. We dig in, as Mike and Lilly join us.

"Care if we sit, too?" Mike asks.

"Not at all. How's the horse doing?" I ask.

"She hates the stall but liked being around other horses. I think they're trying to convince her we're good people, or maybe, she recognizes some of them from wherever they came from," Mike says.

"I was looking up illegal rodeos and racing rings. Everything I've read indicates they work the horses, and then kill them and dump their bodies. Why are they letting these ones live?" I ask.

"Originally, we thought it was someone who had a soft spot for the horses and picked Rock Springs because they had some connections to the town. But the guy they picked up in the sting is local, so he blew that theory out of the water. Though, he insists he was following orders," Greg says.

"Almost like they're playing a game of chicken to see how much they can push before they're caught," Lilly says.

"Yep," Greg agrees.

"Horses have started to go missing closer to Dallas now, according to the reports that are coming in," Miles announces, as he stops at the table.

"So, are they moving away from the area?" I ask.

"Stealing wise, yes. They know we're more on our guard. We thought the horses might stop since we caught the guy who was dropping them here. There was also speculation the horses would be left somewhere new since the missing horses are moving closer to Dallas. That got blown out of the water when the horse showed up the other day. So, we aren't sure," Miles says.

"Any leads at all?" Mike asks.

"There are some whispers of grubstakes betting going on in Dallas. It's supposed to be this super exclusive club with a half million dollar buy in, and you have to know someone to get invited. That's all we got, and can't seem to track anything else down. Generally, the high price clubs like that take better care of their horses, and then sell to members or breed them. Basically, they take better care of the animals." Mile says.

"Normally, stuff like this is underground betting and such. The ones who are gambling addicted, bookies, and many people with warrants out for their arrest," Mike says.

"Yeah, but there isn't even a hint of anything like that happening from Amarillo as far south as Austin. Normally, some of our undercovers would have heard something by now." Miles shakes his head.

"All it takes is one slip up. That's what my dad would have said. It's hard to wait, but the longer it goes on, the bigger chance they will slip up," I say.

"It's the waiting everyone hates," Greg says.

Everyone agrees and starts to head their own way, leaving just Greg and me to finish our food.

"Come on! We're not going to let this put a damper on our day. We can worry about the horses later. Let's have some fun." I say, trying to push the dark cloud away.

"Games as the food settles?" He asks.

I nod and follow him down one of the town's side roads that have been blocked off for the carnival and have the games set up on. Tents and booths feature all kinds of games lining the sides, as people watch and take part.

The first game we play is a water shooting game, and we both lose out to Mac, who wins a cute pink teddy bear for his wife, Sarah.

We cheer on Mike and Lilly at another game, before Greg steps up to one with darts and balloons and wins me the most adorable penguin. It's the perfect keepsake of my time here in Rock Springs this summer.

"Is your stomach settled enough to take on a few rides?" Greg asks as we approach the bumper cars.

"I'm horrible at bumper cars," I say, as we get in line.

"Then, let's get a double, and you can ride with me, and we can go up against Blaze and Riley." He nods towards them, who are a few people ahead of us.

"Sounds like a plan," I say, as the line starts moving, and we grab a car and buckle up.

Greg is a good driver, and once Blaze and Riley realize we're on to them, the fun begins. I don't remember the last time I laughed so freely. At the end, Riley is laughing so hard that she can barely walk and has to lean on Blaze. My stomach and cheeks hurt, and my heart hasn't been this full, since my parents died.

"Tilt-a-Whirl next? It was always my favorite." I ask.

"It's my sister's favorite, too. Let's go," he says.

The line moves fast, and we end up in our own seat with the curved sides, almost like we're in our own little bubble. There's enough space between us to fit another person, but that changes, as soon as the ride starts, and we begin spinning. Before I know it, I'm pressed up against Greg's side, and he has wrapped an arm around me to hold me steady.

I'm leaning into him, and I tell myself it's because I don't have a choice. Even though I can't move, because of the force of the ride, I also know I'm not trying too hard. I'm soaking up having his arm around me, and his body heat surrounding me.

Having him so close makes me achy, and there are feelings between my thighs that I haven't felt before. Not knowing what to do with them, I try to ignore it and focus on his laugh. That backfires because it just makes me ache more.

I'm turned into his side, trying to get my balance back. My nipples harden against my thin bra, as I feel them scrape his side, and it makes me wonder. Can he feel them, too? Then, the ride jerks, and I'm thrown against him again.

My heart is racing, and his hand travels down from my shoulder to my waist and his grip on me tightens. Am I imagining the heat in his eyes? I have to be. There's no way he knows what I'm feeling right now, or how turned on I am.

There's just no way.

The ride starts to slow down, but neither of us moves and puts space between us like we should. Until the attendant comes around to unlock our seat, breaking the spell, we can't take our eyes off each other.

It's only awkward until we're off the ride, but once in the crowd, everything feels back to normal. We ride a few more rides that do the same thing with the force of the ride, pushing us together, and we let it happen, blaming it on the ride when really we don't stop it.

Then, the minute we're off the ride, everything is back to normal.

"How do you feel about the haunted house ride?" He nods towards the building in front of us.

It looks like a haunted house, but instead of walking, you ride a small car fit for just two people.

"I've never been on one, so I'm willing to check it out." The first room on the ride is kind of lame, but I could see how it would scare kids.

The further we get, the darker it gets, and when we get to room three, and things start lunging at the car, I jump, and without thinking, bury my face into Greg's chest. He doesn't hesitate, wrapping his arms around me and holding me close for the rest of the ride.

Until the sunlight peeks through, signaling we're done, I don't move. When the ride slows, we sit up, and again, just watch each other, until the car comes to a complete stop.

By now, the sun is starting to set, casting a golden glow over the carnival.

"It's the perfect time to ride The Ferris Wheel. You up for it?" He asks.

"Let's do it. You know Sage will just drag me here tomorrow, if I don't," I joke.

We get in line and quickly take our seats. The seats are for two people with a bar over it, but the high back curves up, making it impossible for people on the ground to see what people at the top are doing.

We make the slow climb to the top, both of us checking out the carnival. As we rise over the buildings, he starts pointing out different locations around town. Once we reach the top, the view takes my breath away. I'm able to get my phone out and take a few photos, too.

The view is straight down Main Street with the setting sun in the distance, lighting up the sky in beautiful colors.

"It's beautiful." I sigh.

"This is what put this carnival on the map across the state." He says proudly.

"Can we go around again?" I ask.

"Of course." When we get back to the start, he nods to the guy, who lets us go back up again.

"Got connections, huh?" I joke.

"Helps to be the pastor of the church, putting the event on," he winks.

As we get closer to the top again, the colors have changed only slightly, and this time, I just take in the view.

Again, we're stopped at the top, and this time, I look over at Greg, who is studying me. I bite my bottom lip, not sure what to say, and that seems to make the decision for him. He cups my cheek and slowly leans forward.

I know what he's doing, and I don't stop him. I want this. Every nerve in my body is on fire, every fiber in me is screaming to kiss him, and I listen. My heart races, as his soft lips touch mine. When my hands reach up and tangle in his hair, it spurs him on.

His tongue traces my lips, as he pulls me closer to him. My breasts are pressed to his chest, creating a delicious friction with each breath we take. Then, I pull him impossibly close, as I open my mouth for him, and our tongues meet.

Nothing has ever felt so right or so perfect, as him kissing me. It's as if he's making love to my mouth. He pulls back just enough to tilt his head to the other side and continue the kiss. I explore his lips, as he explores mine. The sensations are almost too much, and it causes me to let out a soft moan. His hand on my hip tightens, and he tries to pull me closer, even though there's nowhere for me to go.

When the ride jerks and starts moving again, all my senses come back, and I pull away, like a moth that got too close to the fire. We're both breathing hard, trying to catch our breath, and staring at each other the whole ride down.

As soon as the ride stops, and the attendant opens the bar on our car, I jump up and run. Behind me, I can hear Greg calling my name, but I keep running.

What the hell did I just do?

Chapter 19

Abby

Why does stepping off the plane here in Arkansas feel so wrong? I left the carnival and went right back to the ranch and packed my bags. I said goodbye, once everyone got back, but Sage knew something was wrong.

After that mind-blowing kiss, all I could think about was getting to the Dallas airport as fast as I could, and I took the first flight back.

Even though I had to sit in the airport for three hours, before my flight, I didn't care, but here I am. William didn't ask why I was coming home early but said he'd be here to pick me up. Other than my texts about coming home early, we haven't talked in almost a week, other than a few check-in 'how are you' texts.

So, I take my time walking towards the exit, almost dreading seeing William face-to-face after almost two months. Part of me is expecting one of The Rutherford's to be there because he had something come up.

But there he is, waiting for me with the rest of the people. Looking like he just came from work, because he's still in his black suit. He's handsome, and we can't go out without other girls checking him out. Most girls don't even hide it like they think he will take them right then and there.

Even now, there are a few girls to the side-, staring and giggling at him. He doesn't notice them though, and he doesn't notice me, because he's more interested in what's on his phone. For some reason, I hate that even more than if he had just bailed.

I look around, seeing who else came with him, and find that he's alone. This will be the first time we're alone, just the two of us, and I'm not as nervous as I thought I'd be.

I walk just past the security line and stop and watch him. People pass by, and even someone bumping into him, he doesn't look up. He just keeps reading and typing on his phone. So much for a huge I missed you so much welcome.

Sighing, I hoist my bag higher over my shoulder and walk up to him.

"Thanks for picking me up," I say, and then continue walking to get the rest of my bags.

"Abby!" He says with a hint of amusement in his voice.

"Since I'm sure work is missing you, why don't you just drop me off and get back to it," I say with irritation.

"I took the day off, so we could catch up."

"Didn't look like it." I snap and then regret it. This isn't me.

"I'm sorry. It's been a rough few days, and the flight wasn't good. I had a different homecoming in mind, but you didn't even see me." I say, keeping my voice as light as possible.

Hearing my words, he reaches for my hand and stops me. Then, he spins me around to look at him, and his eyes run over me, concern written all over his face. I get my first good look at him, and he looks tired with dark circles under his eyes. While his face is clean shaven, his almost black hair is slightly messy and longer than normal, like he hasn't had time to get a haircut.

"Come here." He says above a whisper and pulls me in for a hug. He rests his head on top of mine, and while I hug him back, it feels wrong. It doesn't comfort me like it used, too. This hug actually makes my nerves worse, and I want to crawl out of my skin.

So, I give him another squeeze and pull back, offering a smile that I hope doesn't look forced.

"If you have time for lunch, I'm starving," I say. I'm also exhausted because I didn't sleep last night. Then, I had to be at the airport really early this morning, but I can sleep tonight. I keep telling myself that I have a lot to figure out.

"I'm yours for the rest of the day. Look, I'm even putting my cell phone on silent." He pulls his phone out and presses a few buttons.

Then, he helps me with my bags, and we head out to his car. He's nothing short of the perfect gentleman I've always known him to be. At the car, he opens my door and then loads my bags for me.

Once in the car, he even puts on my favorite music station, and when we're out of the busy airport, he holds my hand on the way to our favorite diner. So, why is it I can't stop thinking of Greg? Why does holding William's hand feel so wrong?

When we're seated, I pull out my phone and smile at William.

"I should text them and let them know I got in okay," I say.

He nods and places our drink order, while I send a group text to Sage and her family. Glancing at my unread texts, I see one from Greg. Debating if I should read it, I glance up at William, who is reading the menu, so I turn back to my phone.

Greg: I'm sorry about the way we left things, but I'm not sorry about what happened. That kiss was amazing.

I delete that one. No point in hurting William, if he sees it.

Greg: Sage says you're heading home. Please, let me know you made it okay.

I decide to at least let him know I'm fine.

Me: Just got in and having lunch with William. Hope the rest of the carnival goes well.

Then, I turn my phone on silent and put it back in my purse. We spend our lunch time catching up on everything we missed. He tells me about the big case they took at work, and how he's one of two up for the promotion and all the weird hours he's been working to get it.

Though, he keeps saying the promotion is for us, only it doesn't feel that way. It never did.

I tell him about the carnival and about the cut on my arm, which is healing well. Leaving out The Ferris Wheel and all that happened on it, because I feel guilty about that, and I need to sort through it before I'm ready to talk about it. He catches me up on what's going on at church and with some of our friends as well.

When we get back out to his car, he pauses, before opening the door for me. Then, he takes my hand, pulling me towards him with heat in his eyes. Pinning my back to the car, he leans in to kiss me. Even though he has me pinned to the car in a possessive way, the kiss is soft and passionate, but I feel nothing. Not like the kiss with Greg.

This kiss doesn't give me butterflies, and I don't feel even a slight twinge between my thighs. There's more chemistry sitting in the same room as Greg and not touching than there is in this kiss. Desperate to feel something, I wrap my hands in his hair and pull him closer, allowing myself to melt into this kiss, but I still feel nothing.

When we finally break apart, we're both slightly winded. It's nothing like the gasping for air when I kissed Greg. Williams's eyes are filled with heat, as he stares at me. He doesn't look like he's trying to stop himself from kissing me again. Taking a quick glance down, like I'm straightening my dress, proves that William isn't even hard from the kiss. Not like I felt Greg was. Like I knew he was.

William leans forward and kisses my forehead. "That was the kiss we should have had at the airport." He whispers, before pulling away and opening my door for me to get in the car.

The next few days are spent with The Rutherford's, talking about my trip and getting back into my normal routine. I help make dinner, and we have a movie night. When I attend a church service, it's suddenly the last place I want to be. After going to church in Rock Springs with the charming, old building and all the natural light, this closed off church feels stuffy and suffocating.

Sage and Riley call me at least once a day with updates and to see how I'm doing. They're sending me photos of the ranch and around town. Yesterday, Sage sent a photo she snuck at church with Greg up at the pulpit, giving his sermon. She captioned it 'church isn't the same without you,' but I know what she was trying to do.

Riley is attempting to do the same thing. They're trying to make me miss Rock Springs. Well, they don't have to try. I miss it plenty all on my own. The more time I spend with William, the more confused I am. I was supposed to come back from Rock Springs with clarity and a clear direction of where I was going, only I'm more muddled than ever.

What makes it even worse is I find myself looking forward to lunchtime every day. Like clockwork, at lunch, Greg texts me. It's always a photo of Bluebell and a funny caption. He will also update me on things like how the carnival did, or something going on at church. So today, I scarf down an early lunch and tell Mrs. Rutherford I'm going for a walk. Taking the dogs with me, I head out to the walking trails at the back of the property.

I barely hit the tree line, when the first text comes in.

Greg: Bluebell spent all morning chasing a rabbit around the church, and then came home and passed out on my bed.

The attached photo is of Bluebell, lying on her back asleep with her head hanging over the side of the bed, and her tongue falling out of the side of her mouth.

Me: How is that comfortable?
Greg: I have no idea, but she didn't even move when the microwave went off for my lunch.

Wanting to keep the conversation going, I ask simple questions.

Me: What are you having for lunch?

Greg: Mrs. Willow's mac and cheese casserole. She made two pans of it and put them in my freezer last week. I cooked one of them the other day, and I've been living off it for three days now.

Me: I'm pretty sure that was a party size platter meant for when you have company over.

Greg: Food is fair game anytime. The less I have to cook for just myself, the better.

I send him a laughing emoji, but he doesn't respond back, and I'm not ready for the conversation to end.

Me: How did your sister and her family like the carnival?

Greg: They had fun, and the kids didn't want to leave. They kept asking about you.

A pit forms in my stomach. This is the closest we have come to talking about what happened between us. I know I should change the subject. Actually, I should end the conversation and go back to the house, but I don't.

Me: What did you tell them?

Greg: That you went home early to get ready for classes.

I hate that I put him in the position, especially since I have just over four weeks before school starts back up again. Really, I should have said goodbye to him myself. Heck, I'm regretting not saying goodbye to Greg, but I panicked.

Me: I'm sorry for how I left things.

I don't know what I'm expecting, but when he doesn't text back, my heart sinks. When I turn to go back towards the house, my phone rings. Seeing it's Greg, my hand starts to shake. I shouldn't answer it, I should keep things to texting, but my heart just wants to hear his voice.

"Hello," I answer tentatively.

"Angel." He sighs like he didn't think I'd pick up the phone. "I didn't want to have this conversation via text." He says it so tenderly it almost breaks my heart.

"I'm so sorry, Greg. It was never my intention to put you in a situation, where you had to lie for me." I say, rushing to get the words out before I chicken out.

"Angel, you have nothing to apologize for. This was my fault. I never should have kissed you and put you in this situation."

My heart races, and I feel sick at the thought that he regrets what happened.

"I don't regret it, not one second of it." He says, almost reading my mind.

"It was a great kiss," I whisper into the phone like they might hear me all the way back at the house, which is a good quarter mile away.

"Yeah, it was," I swear I hear a smile in his voice.

Flashes of the kiss with William, pressing me against the door, come to my mind, and suddenly, I can't breathe. I need to stop talking and hang up.

Trembling, I say to him, "I need to get going, but it was great to hear your voice."

"Call anytime." He says before we hang up.

I've never been so confused.

Chapter 20

Abby

I check the GPS again to make sure I'm on the right road and take a deep breath. I'm doing the right thing.

After my call with Greg, I called Sage. She always seems to know what to do. When she suggested I head to Walker Lake, Texas, where her family has a cabin on the lake, and spend a few days clearing my head, I knew that's what I was going to do. The icing on the cake was that she and Colt were going to come up, and we could talk or just have a girl's weekend.

So, that's where I'm heading now. The Rutherford's weren't too happy, seeing as I had just gotten back, and neither was William. But other than our lunch the day he got back and the church, I haven't seen much of him. There was no hesitation on my part. I packed my clothes, and the next morning I was on the road.

The GPS says it's about a ten hour drive, so I left, as soon as the sun was up just before six a.m. With minimal stops, I should make it in time for dinner.

When my phone rings, I screen the call and breathe a sigh of relief, when I see it's Sage.

I answer it with the car's Bluetooth.

"We just got to the cabin. How far out are you?" She asks.

"About four hours."

"Okay, we're going to go to the store and stock the fridge, and I'll have dinner ready. Just call, when you get to Amarillo," she says.

"Perfect. Get ice cream." I say.

"And cookie dough. I know the drill. Drive safe, and we'll see you soon."

We hang up, and about thirty minutes later, I stop to get gas. Then, I check my phone and see Greg's daily text from earlier still unread. Though I was driving and almost pulled over just to answer it, but in the end, decided to wait, until I stopped like now.

I take a deep breath and open it to find a picture of Bluebell and him.

Greg: She isn't the only one who is missing you.

I know I shouldn't respond, and just simply delete the message. I shouldn't be saving the photo to my phone, and I definitely shouldn't be replying to him.

Me: I miss you both, too. More than I can put into words.

Then, I put the phone away, use the restroom, fill up the car, and get back on the road.

• • • ● • ● • • •

At just after five-thirty, I pull into the driveway-. Getting out of the car, I step up on the porch, and Sage's cooking fills the air. I knock, and a moment later, Colt opens the door with a smile on his face.

"Hey, Abby." He greets me with a side hug and then opens the door to let me in, and I involuntarily gasp.

From the front, this place appears to be a little wood cabin near the lake. But looks can be deceiving because the house is long and massive.

"This isn't a cabin!" I say as Sage rounds the corner from where I guess the kitchen is.

"This is Texas. Go big or go home." She shrugs and then hugs me.

"Mom and Dad bought this cabin for the family. The kids had their own room, and now, each couple has their own room, and they're planning some remodeling to make one large grandkids room. Come on, Blaze and Riley said you can stay in their room." She guides me to the far side of the living room.

I notice there are three short hallways off the large open living room, dining room, and kitchen. Each hallway has a door on either side.

She takes me down the first hallway and to the door on the left.

"This is Blaze and Riley's room, and across the hall, is Mac and Sarah's room. They share a bathroom, but since they aren't here, the bathroom is all yours. Colt and I are down the second hallway the door on the left," she says.

Colt comes in and places my bag on the bed. "Get settled and come out, when you're ready. We can give you a tour before we eat," he says.

They leave me alone in my room, which is big enough to be called a small apartment. When I unpack my suitcase and check my phone, I see I have a missed call and a text from Greg.

Greg: I just wanted to hear your voice. Hope you're having a good day.

I don't answer. I promised myself not to reply to him again until I tell Sage everything and get her advice. So, I send William and The Rutherford's a text, letting them know I made it, and then, I plug my phone in and leave out to find Sage and Colt.

"Ready for the house tour?" Sage greets me.

She shows me everyone's bedrooms, the loft, office, massive game room, TV room, and the master suite with the best view. When we step out onto the deck, I'm blown away by the size.

The deck runs the length of the house and faces the lake. It's so long it's broken down into sections. One end has a grill and an outdoor dining area. The other end near the master bedroom has a massive hot tub that could easily fit ten people or more. The center has a fire pit and a large seating area with a lounge chair that will be perfect to lay out under the sun.

There are steps that lead to a path which goes down to the lake, where there's another sitting and grilling area and a dock.

"This place is beautiful," I say.

"It's magical." Sage agrees.

After we eat dinner, Sage holds up the ice cream. "Ready to talk about it?"

"Yeah, let me grab my phone. Might as well let you see the text messages, too."

After I grab my phone, I join them on the deck, as the sun starts to set. There's beauty all around me, but I just can't enjoy it today.

"I'll leave you ladies to it," Colts says.

"Might as well stay. I know Sage will tell you everything anyway, and I could use a man's opinion."

He glances at Sage, who nods. In a few long glides, he's picking Sage up from her chair and placing her in his lap, as he takes over her spot. That's what I want. I know that without a shadow of a doubt.

Once we're seated, I start at the beginning. I tell them everything from my time with Greg, my feelings, the almost kisses, lunches, how he took care of me when I hurt my arm, and down to the kiss.

Then, I tell them about William. How the lack of communication close to the festival bothered me, him much time he's taking working for the promotion, and my feelings about it. I go on to tell them about the greeting at the airport, our lunch, and his kiss, and the lack of feelings.

I show them Greg's texts and pictures and tell them about the phone call yesterday that I had right before I called Sage. When I'm done, even Colt is eating the last of the Ice cream.

"Well, damn," Sage says.

"From the outside looking in, the answer is easy. You go with the person whose kiss has sparks. The one who you want to be with, but are too afraid to admit it to yourself," Colt says.

"I have to agree with him. From where I'm sitting, it's not even a competition. What is really holding you back?" Sage asks.

"My parents would love William. He's the type of guy they always talked about me dating."

"From the little amount of time I spent with your parents, I know without a doubt they would want you to be happy. They wouldn't want you to marry someone you didn't have feelings for. Besides, Greg is a pastor whose church loves him. You don't think they would approve?" She asks.

I don't answer. I don't have to, because they both know that, of course, my parents would approve. Not only is Greg sweet, but he's kind, helps anyone without question, he's a pastor, close with his family, treats me like gold, and I'm not even his.

"I got offered a job in Rock Springs working with Riley and Megan's doctor," I say, barely above a whisper.

Sage and Colt look at each other, as I look out over the lake.

"There's a school twenty minutes from the ranch... if you needed a sign, I think this was it," Sage says.

"Why don't you sleep on it? Then tomorrow, we can make a pro and con list, while we go swimming, and you girls can get some sun," Colt says.

"A pro con list on which guy to pick?" I give a humorless laugh.

"No, that seems pretty cut and dry. It's a list to determine if you take the job in Rock Springs or stay in Arkansas to finish school," he smiles.

· · · ● ●· ● ● · · ·

As promised, we spent the morning in the lake. While Sage and I swam, we talked and yelled out items for Colt to add to the list. After coming in for lunch, we spent time on the deck, getting some sun and continuing the pro con list.

When Colt went inside to make some dinner, Sage and I jumped in the lake again to cool off. It provided me an opportunity to clear my mind of both men and the possible move. To distract me, Sage keeps telling me about her favorite stories from growing up and visiting the lake house.

"Hey, girls. Sarah texted there's a food show going on downtown starting tomorrow. Want to go check it out?" Colt asks.

Sage looks at me, and I nod. Anything to get my mind off everything.

"Okay, Abby, answer this without thinking about it. Who do you imagine being downtown with tomorrow?" Sage asks.

Without thinking, I answer, "Greg."

"Well, you have your answer." Sage smiles and then starts walking back to the house.

If only it were that easy.

I don't get much sleep that night, because every time I do, I have nightmares of making a choice that kills the one I don't choose. Though I know this choice isn't life or death, but apparently, my brain wants me to think it is.

The next day at the event downtown we sample some great food, walk the shops, stroll by the lake, and talk to some locals. The entire time all I can think about is how I wish Greg were here, and how much he'd love the lake and chatting with people.

When his daily text comes in, this time, it's a photo of just him with the Dallas skyline in the background.

Greg: Spending the day in Dallas, talking with my friend Ian. He's the pastor of a church here. I'll be stopping to get some fudge on my way home.

Seeing Sage and Colt talking with someone, I snap a photo of me with the food tents in the background.

Me: Fudge sounds great, but I've been sampling food all day. I'm stuffed!

Greg: Looks like a fun day date.

I laugh, truly laugh for the first time in days. I could let him stew in his jealousy, but I decide to put him out of his misery.

Me: William is at work, and I'm here with some friends.

Greg: Happy to be back in Arkansas?

Me: I don't know, since I'm not in Arkansas.

When Sage and Colt walk back over, I take a photo of the three of us with the lake in the background and send it to him.

He doesn't answer, so I pocket my phone, and we check out the arts and crafts section, before heading back to the lake house. I actually have some fun and forget about the big decision I have to make, and all about the drama, as we have dinner and a movie night.

Before bed, I check my phone, and that's when I see his reply.

Greg: Why are you back in Texas, Angel?

Me: Needed some space to think.

Chapter 21

Greg

M y sister is only here for another night, but she cornered me, insisting we have a night to ourselves to talk. I guess, she's realized I'm not myself and is worried about me. Apparently, I wasn't hiding how I felt as well as I thought I was.

So, after dinner, her husband took the kids inside for a movie night, and she and I are spending time on the back porch.

Once again, I check my phone, but there's nothing new from Abby, not since our conversation where she said she needed space to think. I can only hope she's recognizing her feelings for me and needed a break from William.

"Oh, get out of your head and tell me what's going on." My sister says.

So, I sit back and tell her everything. My feelings for Abby, the carnival, the kiss, our texts, since she left, the phone call, and the conversation earlier today. I don't leave out any detail and tell her the same way I laid it all out for Ian, too.

Then, I sit back and wait for her to tell me I'm crazy, she's taken, I need to move on, find a nice girl, or maybe, try looking closer to Dallas. Only what comes out of my sister's mouth is nothing like what I expected.

"Do you love her?" She asks.

Though she's a bit more direct than Ian was, but even his question surprised me.

It takes me a minute to form my answer. Not because I'm unsure of my feelings, but because I'm so stunned that this is what my sister is asking.

"Yes. I've never been more certain of anything in my life." I answer honestly.

She nods and looks out into the distance. We both take a moment to think because I know what I want to do, and what I should do. I should stay here and wait for Abby to make up her mind. What I want to do is to race to her, fall to my knees, and beg her to pick me.

"So, what are you going to do about it?" She swings her eyes back to me to watch my reaction. Though, I have no idea how to react.

"Nothing. This is something she has to figure out on her own. You know what. I can't make this choice for her, as much as I want to show up at her door, throw her over my shoulder, and bring her back here, and not let go."

That image flashes in my mind for a brief moment, and I smile. How mad she would be at me. That little spark, when she knows she's right.

"But you need to show her why she should pick you."

"I have been. I've showed her how I'd treat her, and I've stayed in contact but not too pushy. Even when it felt like she was pushing me away, I still texted. Even if it was just about Bluebell."

At the mention of her name, she sits up and looks at me, so I reach down and pet her. What I haven't told Abby is that even Bluebell seems sad. She misses her as much as I do.

My sister gives me a look like she doesn't believe me like she thinks I'm not doing something I should be doing.

"Listen, I know she isn't happy with William. It was very clear, while she was here. But she has to decide to be happy for herself. I don't ever want to catch her wondering what if I stuck it out with William, until after his promotion, or another month, or if I did this instead of that. It would kill me."

"Well, Sage is there talking to her now. Maybe, she and Colt can talk some sense into her." My sister says hopefully.

"That's all I can wish for, but I'm not holding my breath. I'll wait for her for as long as it takes because she's my one. I don't plan to marry a fill in just to please anyone." I level her with a glare.

"Message received. Just how do you plan to tell your little, old church ladies, though?"

"I don't think they would meddle, even more than you would."

• • • ● • ● • • •

Abby

Sage and Colt went home a few days ago, and I decided to stay and take my time, relaxing by the lake. I turned my phone off and developed a routine. It's essential to keep my mind off Greg and focus on what I want.

In the morning, I get a cup of coffee to wake up, then take a large to-go cup of coffee and walk around the lake.

After my walk, I spent time reading all the books that were piling up on my to-be-read list. Then, I read until lunch, ate, went for a swim in the lake, and lay in the sun, listening to some music. After that, I spent time in the movie room, watching movies, until dinner, when I head into town and eat at the diner.

Austin, who runs the diner, has been great to talk with. She shares all the town gossip with me, which I find entertaining. I'll stay until after dark, and then come home and read some more out on the deck under the stars and watch others near the lake.

This is what I should have been doing during summer break. It's a simple boring life and one that I crave. That's when it hits me. I want to be a midwife, and on my off time, this is what I want. I want to be able to relax and do something for me, read, walk, or swim. With William, that won't happen.

He's made it clear he wants a family and wants me to be home with them and be a church wife. Be by his side and help him climb the ladder of one promotion after another. Things won't get better after he gets this promotion. It will just get worse.

In that moment, I know I don't want that life, which means I need to end things with William. Though, I will do in person, as he deserves it. So, I pack a few things, knowing I'll be coming back, and the next day, I get on the road towards Arkansas.

As I get closer to town, I call him to see if he can meet me.

"Abby, I have to get these papers done for the meeting tomorrow," he says.

"Can I stop by the office? I'll bring dinner and not stay more than a few minutes, but I need to see you," I say.

He hesitates a moment, and I think he knows what's coming.

"Okay, I'll place an order at the Italian place by the office for you to pick up. See you soon." His voice is soft, but not the strong, sure voice I'm used to.

I pick up the food and send a text to The Rutherford's as well. I'll go there after this. On the way here from Walker Lake, I thought a lot of what I want and need.

Walking into his office, I'm surprised by how many people are still here at seven at night. This is how it will always be, and I'm not okay with this kind of lifestyle. I don't want to be a work widow, not for all the money in the world. It's just further solidified that I'm making the right choice.

I tap on the door frame of his office, and he looks up at me with a sad, tired smile. I hand him the food and don't even sit down.

"How was the lake?" He asks, trying to start the conversation.

"Peaceful. I got a lot of thinking done about where I want my life to go, and what I want to do."

"And you're here to tell me it doesn't include me." He says his tone still soft, but flat, almost emotionless.

He's not mad, but he knew this was coming. Maybe, William knew the day he picked me up at the airport, but I'm sure he knew it before I did.

"I'm sorry, William. You're the exact guy I want to be with, but the spark I need isn't there, and this isn't the life I see ahead of me." I wave my arms out around his office.

"You're going back to Rock Springs?" He asks.

"I think I am. It feels like home, and I'm more part of a community there than I am here."

He stands up and rounds his desk. He pulls me in for a hug. "You're everything I want to, but your dreams are a lot bigger than this town, and I don't ever want to hold you back."

I return the hug. That was much easier than I expected. We say our goodbyes before I head downstairs and back to my car. One down and one to go.

My next stop is The Rutherford's and to thank them for everything they have done for me and let them know William and I ended things. But it's time to tell them I'm taking a different route, explain about the job offer in Rock Springs, and how I'm transferring schools there to take it.

They're supportive of me and let me stay the night. All my stuff fits in my car, and the next morning, I'm back on the road to Walker Lake. It's time to start putting things into motion because I need to have everything in order to talk to Greg.

Once I cross over the Oklahoma state line, I call Sage.

"So, is your offer to stay with you still open?" I ask.

"Always. You're moving here for good?" She asks.

"Yes, I have to get a few things in order, but keep this to yourself, until I get there."

"You don't want Greg to know?"

"No, I want to tell him myself. I don't know if it will go anywhere, but after the way I left, I need to apologize in person."

"Okay, just let me know when you'll be here, and I'll have your room ready. You can stay in the guest master, as there's plenty of room for us to add a desk, so you can do schoolwork."

"Perfect. Talk soon."

I spend the next hour, debating calling Greg. Though we haven't talked in days, he kept sending texts, even when I didn't reply.

It's just before lunch, and I know his daily text will come in anytime, so I decide to beat him to the punch and call him.

"Hey, I was starting to worry, when I didn't hear from you," he says.

"I turned my phone off because I had a lot of thinking to do. How is Bluebell?" I ask.

"Lazy as ever. Spends all morning running around, and then sleeps all day. She likes going out in town with me, though."

"How's everything?" I ask, and now wish I had better topics planned to talk about, because I'm not ready to share my plans, and I don't want to give too much away.

"Good, I picked up some plants to do some landscaping in front of the church this weekend. All these abandoned horses at the church really tore it up, and I figure it's time to repair it."

Just like that, we start talking about plants and colors and ideas for the landscaping. An idea starts to form, and when we hang up, I decide the rest of my plans can wait until tomorrow. Though, I don't want to wait and would rather start making plans now.

As soon as I get into town, I pick up dinner from the diner and take it back to the cabin to eat, and pass out.

The next day, I spend it making phone calls, getting my school stuff transferred, setting up the new job, and filling out all the paperwork for that. It takes all day to get everything prepared for transferring schools, but it's all done.

Before I start my new normal, I think I deserve one more day of my lazy routine.

Chapter 22

Greg

I 've spent all morning working on the church landscaping. I thought it would be a great distraction to keep my mind off Abby, but while my hands work, my mind is constantly on her.

What has she been thinking about? Why was she out without William? Did they break up? I've stared at the picture she sent me more than I should, and it's the start of my dreams every night since. My dreams are turning to her and me out on that date.

I miss her but hearing her voice the other day was worth the time apart. I know it wasn't my imagination, but she seemed happier, lighter, and more herself. The self she was here when she let go.

That's how I want her, happy and carefree. Even if that means she isn't here with me, but knowing she's happy makes it easier.

I get so lost in thought that I don't hear a car pull up behind me until the door slams shut. Then, I stand up and wipe the dust off my hands, before turning around. What I expect to see is one of the church ladies or one of the local ranchers.

What I wasn't prepared to find was Abby, standing in front of me. While she looks shy and a little nervous, the smile on her face reaches her eyes. She's in a blue sundress, and her hair is done in loose curls. It's a casual look, and she could be going to church on Sunday, or just running around town-. But whatever she's doing, she looks drop dead gorgeous.

"What are you doing here?" I'm scared to move because every fiber in my body wants to pull her in and kiss her until she forgets everything else. Another part of me is worried she's here to tell me goodbye, and this will be the last time I see her.

Turning to look at the car that's full of boxes, she says, "I'm moving in with Sage at the ranch, but I wanted to stop by here first."

She's moving here.

Does this mean we actually have a shot to see how things go between us, or is she going to do the long-distance thing with William? I clench my fists and will my body not to move just yet.

"You're moving here?" I have to make sure I heard her right and wasn't imagining it.

"Yeah. I transferred to the school here and took the job offer Dr. Shelly made me at the wedding."

"How did William take that?"

I watch her for any sign that I should have hope. Hope that she chose me. Hope that I finally get to call her mine.

"Better than I expected. He knew things were off between us too, so it was a lot easier than I expected to break up with him."

I close my eyes and take a deep breath. I prayed for this every night, but I never thought I'd be here where she's just in reach.

"I'm sorry it didn't work out. Are you okay?"

"Are you sorry?" She cocks her head to the side.

"Of course, I am. Even if you knew it was coming, and he wasn't right for you, it's still never easy to end a relationship."

"I've had plenty of time to think and plan. I know what I want, and I don't want to waste any more time." She takes a step towards me.

"What do you want?"

"You." Then, she's running towards me and launches herself into my arms.

I'm caught off guard, but still manage to catch her, and then her arms go around my neck, and her lips land on mine. She kisses me, and everything feels right in my world again. It's like I've been sleeping, since our kiss on The Ferris Wheel, and now, I'm brought back to life again with this kiss.

"I love you, Greg." She pulls back from the kiss just enough to look up at me.

"I love you too, Angel, so much," I whisper, and then kiss her again.

I run my hand up and down her back because I can't believe she's here, and I just need to reassure myself she's real. Though I'm scared this is another one of my dreams, and I'm going to wake up in a dark room still without her. I don't think my heart could handle it.

"Take me to your place." She whispers against my lips, and I turn and guide her to the passenger's seat of her car, buckle her in, and take her keys. I drive us to my place at the back of the property and park her car, where it won't be visible from the church.

The moment we're inside the house, my lips are back on hers, but this time, she takes control, and she's walking me backward. I let her lead, as I get lost in the kiss. Her soft lips on mine are my own personal slice of heaven. When I finally look up, we're in my room.

I stop to look at her and make sure she wants this.

"Abby," I sigh before her lips are back on mine, and her hands move under my shirt and up my sides, causing me to shiver.

"I've given this plenty of thought, and I think we have danced around for far too long, don't you?" She says.

I nod to agree with her because it feels like speaking will break this moment.

"This is my first time, but it's what I want." She says, before kissing me again.

I have a war going on in my head. As a church leader, I teach the kids to avoid premarital sex, and this is exactly what I'm getting ready to do. Also, I know their parents wouldn't want them to find out about this. In the next minute, my head is saying they will never find out.

My heart is yelling at my brain, this is our girl, and we're going to marry her, as soon as I can get her to walk down the aisle. Then, my mind says I should wait and put a stop to this, but when her lips are on mine, the thought goes away, and the torture of not having her is too much.

My nightly sexy dreams of her are a pale comparison to her lips on mine, and her luscious body fits against me perfectly. We are only kissing, but I'm ready to fall over the ledge, and I don't think walking away from her right now is even a possibility.

Removing our shoes, we climb up on the bed, lying on our sides pressed together. There's no way to hide how hard I am, and I know she feels it because she's grinding on me. Though, I'm not sure she realizes it.

Then, I run my hand up the soft skin of her leg, under her dress, and to the edge of her panties. I break the kiss to watch her face for any hesitation, as I slowly pull her dress up, but all I see is the same heat I know is reflected back in my eyes.

She sits up without breaking eye contact, and in a flash of movement, whips the dress over her head, and it floats to the ground. The second the fabric hits the floor, my eyes dart back to Abby, who is now in front of me in a white lace bra and panty set, and I suddenly feel overdressed.

When I stand to remove my shirt and pants, her eyes are glued to me, making me even hotter. While I'm undressing, I keep my eyes on her, taking in her milky skin, her hourglass body, and every delectable inch I can't wait to get my hands on.

"You understand what it means if we take this step?" I ask her, as I remove my jeans.

She nods, but I want to be clear.

"It's mean you're mine. We can date, but I plan for you to be my wife. Later, we can talk out the details. However, you want to make it work, we can decide. But if we do this, marriage is the endgame." I stare her down, not wanting to miss even the smallest reaction.

"That's what I want." She sighs and looks up at me.

"Don't move."

I head to the bathroom to get a condom. Though I always have them on hand, it's not that I expected to ever use one myself. As much as I preach to wait to have sex until you're married, I'd rather the older teens be safe, so they know they can always come to me for things like condoms if needed.

Walking back into the room with an almost naked Abby on my bed knocks the wind out of me. She's so beautiful, and right here and now, she's finally mine.

I couldn't speak if I tried, so I climb in bed in my boxer briefs and kiss her and pray the kiss says everything I can't find the words to say.

Her hands run down my back, causing electric shocks to rock my body, as I start gliding my kisses down her neck. Finding her bra in my way, I slide it off, until her perfect round breasts are bare to me. I can tell she's fighting not to cover them, as she grips the sheets.

"You're beautiful," I whisper, taking her nipple in my mouth. The harder I suck on it, the louder she moans. This woman was made for me, and I love it, revel in it. Unhooking her bra and tossing it to the floor, I move to the other nipple, giving it the same attention and soaking up her moans.

As I kiss down her belly, she tries to pull me back up to her mouth.

"Greg." She pleads and locks her legs together just as I get to the tops of her panties.

"Angel, I want you hot and ready for me." I kiss the tops of her thighs, as I slide my hands along her legs, trying to get her to relax.

When I slide into her the first time, I want to have tasted her and to have her scent on me.

"Angel, I want this to hurt as little as possible, which means making you as wet as possible."

Her chest heaves, as she tries to catch her breath, but she nods at me, and her legs loosen. When I gently push them apart, I can see how soaked her panties are. Leaning in, I put my nose to them, soaking in her musky scent with the hint of flowers on her delicate skin.

"Angel," I whisper, and she relaxes again. I slide her panties off her and take in the sight of her naked in my bed. It makes me so hard my cock is screaming at me to slide into her, but I know if I do that now I'll hurt her. So, I'll have to take it slow, no matter that it's killing me.

When I lick her clit, her hips jerk from sensation, and she grips the sheets with intensity. I run my finger over her slit and let her juices coat it before I slowly slide it into her. She's so tight on just one finger; I wonder how I'll ever fit into her.

Giving her clit special attention, I continue to stretch her and work a second finger into her. She keeps moaning, but when I suck hard on her clit-, her hips jerk, and she grips my hair, instead of the sheets, trying to hold me in place. As if there's anywhere else I'd rather be.

Now I just need her to cum, so I hook my fingers, and I know the moment I find that spot inside her because she pulls on my hair and screams my name. A few thrusts over it, and she's cumming on my fingers.

Her pussy is fluttering and gripping my fingers so tight, I get harder thinking about what that will that feel like on my cock. And I can't wait to find out. I'm barely holding on now, as I sit up and remove my boxers, which have a huge wet spot on them from all the cum my cock leaked. I slide the condom on and join her on the bed again.

"You sure about this, Angel?" I ask to make sure she hasn't changed her mind.

"So sure." She pulls me down for a kiss, as I settle between her thighs.

I kiss her hard, and when I know she's distracted, I start to slide into her. She's so warm and wet that, when I bump up against her virginity, I have to stop and bury my head in her neck.

"I have a secret for you, Angel." I lean up and whisper in her ear, before nipping at her earlobe.

"What's that?" She gasps.

"It's my first time, too," I tell her, as I thrust into her, breaking through her hymen and sliding all the way in.

The only thing that stops me from cumming on the spot is her squeal of pain and her nails, digging into my back.

Taking a moment, I kiss her, while I use all my self-control not to move until she relaxes.

As she starts to let go, she wiggles her hips.

"You okay?" I ask as I look into her eyes.

"I feel so full. I think I need you to move." She says, wiggling her hips again.

That I can do. I pull back and slide into her again. The friction is unlike anything I have ever felt. Then, I grip her hands in mine, hold them over her head, and continue to thrust into her.

This is a connection we will only have with each other. While it's something I never expected, it solidifies my statement earlier that she's mine now, and there's no walking away from this. I can't believe she saved this amazing gift for me, and I know I have to do right by her.

My lower back starts tingling, and I know I'm not going to last much longer. I slide one hand between us and start rubbing her clit. Her grip on me tightens, and the pain only intensifies the pleasure of being inside of her.

"Cum for me, Angel. Let me feel your pleasure from the inside out." I groan, and a moment later, her body locks, and her pussy clamps down on me so hard that I swear I blackout. As her orgasm rolls through her, it feels like her body is trying to suction me. Then, I'm cumming in long, hard pulls, and I've never felt this before.

It feels like it's never going to end, and in that moment, I don't want it, too. The pleasure that ripples through my body is so intense, that if I didn't use the last of my control to move to the side, I would have crushed Abby.

It takes a few minutes for us both to recover.

This moment is something I'll always remember. I'm lying with Abby in my arms, and everything is perfect. I trace her arm, as she snuggles in closer to me. When the world around me starts to return with all the questions I should have asked her, before we fell into bed, come rushing in, and I blurt out the first thing that comes to mind.

"All your stuff fit in your car?" I ask.

"Yeah, I didn't have much. When my parents died, I put a lot of stuff in storage."

"I wish I could have you move in here. I want all the time I can get with you, but I think the church might have something to say about that."

"Yeah, they would. But don't think I won't be over all the time. Your porch is the perfect place to study when I start classes again." She kisses my chest. "But it definitely wouldn't be appropriate for me to move in here."

"Neither is what we just did, but I plan to do it again and again." I kiss the top of her head.

"Well then, I guess we will be doing some sneaking around. How are your ninja skills?"

Chapter 23

Abby

2 Months Later

I wasn't joking about having to sneak around with Greg. Everyone was more than happy when we announced we were dating, and Greg introduced me to everyone at church, as his girlfriend that Sunday.

The church ladies were thrilled but made it clear they would be watching us because they weren't very happy about how much they missed between us. They said we were too good at hiding it.

When I wasn't in school, it was easier to sneak around. But since school started up again last month, we have had to be a bit more cunning. Greg would stay with me since my room was on the other end of the house from Sage and everyone else.

It worked great for about a week until Megan and Hunter were up with Willow, who was teething and caught him sneaking out of the house at five a.m. to make his 6:30 service.

They didn't care, but I kept getting the looks from everyone after that. So, Greg cleared out the garage, so that I could park my car in there when I stayed overnight.

Now, I'm packing for our camping weekend. He got his friend, Ian, to come and do Sunday service, and we're going to go camp. I'm debating what to pack to sleep in when his sister calls. When she found out that I moved back to Rock Springs for him, we became fast friends.

"Hey, girl. You ready for this weekend?" She asks.

"Yes, but what do you take for PJs camping?"

"Me, as a married woman? Nothing, but for you take layers, pants, tank tops, shirts, and a hoodie because you don't know how cold it might get."

"Thanks." I walk to my closet and grab the items she mentioned.

"How's school?"

"School's been good. I was at a birth with Dr. Shelly last weekend, and I correctly answered all her questions. So, she said at the next delivery I could deliver the baby, so long as there are no complications."

"That's great!"

"Yeah, if I had stayed in Arkansas, I wouldn't be this close to having hands-on experience yet. At the practice, I was going to be shadowing the doctor or midwife for a good month, before I even got close to a patient."

We talk a few more minutes before Sage knocks on my door.

"Hey, Greg is downstairs."

I hang up with his sister and double check my bags, before taking them downstairs with me.

"Angel." Greg greets me with a side hug and a kiss on the top of my head.

We haven't shown a lot of affection in public outside of some hugs, forehead kisses, and hand holding. I'm okay with that, as I like having that side of him just to myself, and I'm pretty sure he feels the same way.

He takes my bag and leads me out to his truck-, where Bluebell greets me. She had claimed the middle of his bench seat. It's been her seat, since day one, but when she lies down with her head in my lap, I'm perfectly okay with it.

"So, tell me about this super-secret camping spot." He's been keeping the spot under wraps, so I have no idea where we're going.

"It's actually on the back of Ford's property. We went fishing out there last month, and the whole time, I kept thinking that I can't wait to show it to you, so he's letting us hang out there this weekend."

"Remind me to thank him, when I see him next time." I smile, and roll down the windows, enjoying the wind. Greg reaches over, turns the radio up, and then takes my hand in his.

Once we get on the dirt road, Bluebell perks up. As the dust starts flying, we turn the radio down and close up the windows.

A few more turns and we're onto trails that are barely there. We have to open two gates with a key Greg has, and then we park at the end of the road.

"The spot is about a hundred yards down that path. It will open right up," Greg says, as we get out.

Bluebell jumps down and starts exploring, but as always, keeping us in sight.

When I reach in to take one of the bags, Greg stops me by taking his hand in mine and bringing it up to his mouth. He places a light kiss there.

"I got it. I can make more than one trip." He says softly, before leaning in to kiss my cheek.

But I turn my head at the last moment, and his lips land on mine. Then, I wrap a hand around the back of his neck and pull him in closer for a deeper kiss.

When I pull away just a moment later, with a smile on my lips, I know I won't win this argument, before I even speak.

"You can make as many trips as you want, but I'm going to carry something on my way to the camping spot." Then, I grab the bag I tried to pick up before.

Finding it lighter than expected, I grab a second bag and turn to walk the path he pointed out-. Bluebell is right at my feet happy to explore a new area with me.

As we round the bend, the trees open up to a beautiful lake. There's a small meadow between us and the water. It's the perfect spot to camp and has been used many times, as evidence of the fire pit and charcoal grill next to a fairly flat part.

"It's perfect, right?" Greg asks as he walks up behind me.

I smile at him over my shoulder, "Yeah it is."

We walk to the area where it's clear tents have been set up, before and put our bags down.

"I'm going to go grab the cooler, and then I'll put up the tent," Greg kisses my cheek.

Laughing to myself, I get started setting up the tent. This isn't my first rodeo. I did plenty of camping trips with the church, so I know what I'm doing. By the time Greg comes back, I have the stakes in the ground, and the tent more than half set up facing the lake.

Greg looks over at me and then shakes his head. "Is there anything you can't do?"

"When I find something, I'll let you know."

"How about you let me take that over, and you go get ready for a swim?" He says.

"Deal."

I wore my swimsuit under my clothes, so I make eye contact with him and start stripping off my dress. His eyes heat, as he watches my every move. When he sees the bikini I'm wearing under my clothes, he's on me before my dress even hits the ground.

"Please, tell me this isn't what you wear when you go swimming." He growls against my lips.

"You don't like it?" I ask.

"Angel, I love it, but I don't want other men seeing you like this."

I smile against his lips and kiss him again. "It's new and just for you. I'm normally way more covered up when I go swimming."

"Good," he says, palming my ass and grinding his cock into me. "If we start now, we will never get the tent set up."

He groans and backs away, "Go get in the water, Angel."

I take mercy on him and wade into the water until most of my body is covered. Then, I turn and watch him finish setting up the tent. Every so often he turns to look at me, but the moment he's finished, he strips down to his swim shorts and joins me in the water.

He pulls me to him, and I wrap my legs around his trim waist and look into those whiskey colored eyes of his.

We continue to stare into each others eyes, neither of us moving.

"I love you, Abby," he says.

This isn't the first time we have said these words together, but the meaning feels so much more intense right now. The heat in his voice makes my whole body tingle.

"I love you too," I say, barely above a whisper.

"I had this all planned out. The perfect weekend, but right now, like this," he just shakes his head, not saying anything. I kiss him softly, hoping it gets him out of his head.

"I've never met anyone like you," he continues. "You're smart, driven, and beautiful. You have an amazing heart, and watching you light up, as you work with Dr. Shelly, makes me so happy. While I want you to keep working and doing what you love, I also want to be there with you and support you any way I can."

My heart starts racing, as my eyes start to sting, and my throat gets tight, as I fight back the tears.

"I want you to be my wife, but I don't want you to give up anything to do it. I want to organize festivals and help the church with you, but I don't want you to drop everything to do it. Be a midwife, and only do what you want to with the church. I want you happy first and always." He stares into my eyes to get his point across.

"Marry me, Abby. Be my wife and let me be by your side and help all your dreams come true."

This is the last thing I expected this weekend, but I know what I want. It's the choice I made when I moved here, but I didn't make that choice lightly. He made it clear before we made love the first time, we would be here and soon.

"Yes!" I say with a happy smile on my face.

I've never seen such a big smile on Greg's face, but it only lasts a moment, before he's kissing me again. Then, right there in the water, he slides the tops of my bathing suit to the side and exposes my breasts. He lifts me further out of the water and takes my nipple into his mouth and sucks hard, causing me to cry out.

I'm so lost in the sensations of the cool lake water and his hot mouth on my breast, I don't realize we're moving back to the shore until my back hits the ground. He's laid me down on the small beach at the water's edge, our feet still partly in the water.

The second my back hits the sand, his hand is down my bathing suit bottoms and running through my slit. His thumb circles my already sensitive clit, and my back arches up into him.

"I love how sensitive you are for me. Angel, you don't know how hard that makes me," he whispers into my ear.

The more we're together, the dirtier Greg has started to talk. I love seeing this amazing church pastor every Sunday, knowing how dirty he is in bed, but only for me. It's the biggest turn on.

"What were you thinking about just now? Your pussy gripped my fingers so hard," he whispers, before pulling my bottoms to the side. His cock is already at my entrance, and I didn't even feel him pull his trunks down.

He thrusts into me and holds still. "Tell me."

"You. How you're the picture-perfect pastor every Sunday for the town, but only I get this dirty side of you."

He starts a slow drag in and out of me, as he gives me a dry laugh.

"If they knew what I was doing to you right now, even as my fiancé, they would chase me out of town."

His thrusts get a bit quicker with each word until he's pounding in and out of me, almost like he's mad at himself.

"Then maybe, we should have a really short engagement, and then it won't matter if they find out, not that they will," I say against his lips before he kisses me again.

"The shorter the better. I want you in my bed every night, in my arms, and I don't want to hide it anymore," he says, as he hooks his arm under my knee and pulls my leg up, so he can get deeper and thrust in to me harder.

"Because I'm never going to get enough of this. I want to take you in every inch of our home, and all over town. I'm not going to hide how much I love you, so get ready for an insane amount of PDA. I'll make Sage and Colt look shy."

"Yes." I gasp, as he angles his hips to hit my clit with each thrust.

The thought of him holding me in his arms, walking up to be in a crowd from behind and wrapping his arms around me, kissing my neck, and not being shy about it turns me on like nothing else has. So much so, just a few more thrusts, and I'm falling over the edge, screaming his name, not even caring if anyone can hear us.

When he tenses up a moment later, a feeling I've never felt before floods me. His hot cum shoots into me and starts dripping out, which causes another mini orgasm at the feel of him filling me.

He buries his head in my neck and catches his breath, before pulling out of me.

"Shit, we didn't use a condom. I'm so sorry, Angel, I wasn't thinking."

"Even more of a reason for a short engagement." I shrug, sitting up and readjusting my bathing suit.

I don't even get a look at our surroundings before he's pulling me back into the water and running his hands over every inch of me

"Can't have that sand getting anywhere it shouldn't be." He whispers against my lips.

I relax into him and rest my head on his shoulder. That's when I see Bluebell laying on the ground with her back to us facing the trail like she's on guard against anyone who might try to sneak up on us. But more than likely, she just didn't want to watch us, can't blame her.

But the moment his finger grazes my over sensitive clit, I gasp.

"Give me one more, and then I'll go make you dinner, while you lay out in the sun and read," he says.

It doesn't take long, before the pain of it being too many turns into pleasure, and I explode on his fingers. He carries me to the tent where I'm unable to move, as he makes dinner.

This is my idea of the perfect weekend.

Epilogue
Savannah

It's been a while, since I've been home to see my family. My sister particularly. Now seems like a great time, getting ready for Christmas. It has nothing to do with the fact that I was ordered by my label to take a break and get out of the spotlight.

Tours are hard, a new city every night, the hot lights on stage, the sound checks, and lack of privacy. This break is coming at the perfect time. I cringe because it sounds like a lie to even my own ears.

I loved being on tour. The band I was opening for, 3 Stevens, was probably the best band you could hope to have your first tour with. They took care of the people on tour with them, and they made sure I had other girls around me, so I wasn't stuck on a bus full of sweaty men day in and day out.

As I get off the plane in the Dallas airport, I head to the first shop I see and grab a bottle of water. But I cringe when I see my face splashed all over the gossip's rags. On every one of the magazines, they're pairing me with the lead singer of 3 Stevens, who is married.

Happily married.

His wife and I are friends. Well, we were, until this happened.

One photo and some strangers spin on it, and you learn really quickly who your friends are. When they believe some paparazzi over you, it's a hard pill to swallow. Now all of the sudden, I'm labeled as "too much drama" and told to go home, until the gossip dies down. This sucks because I'm going to miss three huge shows, leading up to Christmas.

I pay for my water, keeping my face down, and if the cashier recognizes me, she doesn't say a word. Hopefully, she doesn't. Because I'd like to keep my location secret, as much as possible.

Still, the idea of coming to spend some time with my sister, Lilly, and her new husband, Mike, on their horse ranch in a small town in Texas has its appeal. The only downside being the 'nice guy' Lilly has been telling me she wants to hook me up with. I don't have the heart to tell her no, so I just kept saying next time I was in town, which is now.

Mom and Dad are on some Christmas cruise this year, so visiting them wasn't an option, and I just didn't feel like spending Christmas alone.

So here I am.

Ready to spend Christmas in Rock Springs, a small-town that goes a bit Christmas crazy.

I round the corner and instantly see Mike and Lilly, waiting for me. They don't see me, because they only have eyes for each other. It's great to see them still so in love after almost a year together.

I thought I had that once, and I couldn't have been more wrong. Now, I just don't have time. No one wants to wait around on you, while you're on tour eight months out of the year. But big hits are my dream, and sometimes, that means making some sacrifices to reach it.

When Lilly finally sees me, she lights up, and they both welcome me into a hug. No doubt they have seen the papers by now, but I know they won't mention it, until I do.

I guess it's about to be a very long and uncomfortable ride to the ranch.

• • • ● • ● • • • •

Get the next book in Rock Springs Series. <u>The Cowboy and His Christmas Rockstar</u>. This is Ford and Savannah's story!

• • • ● • ● • • •

Read the Rock Springs Texas series from the beginning with <u>The Cowboy and His Runaway</u>.

• • • ● • ● • • •

Do you like Cowboys? Military Men? Best friends brothers? What about sweet, sexy, and addicting books?
If you join Kaci Rose's Newsletter you get these books free!
<u>https://www.kacirose.com/free-books/</u>

Connect with Kaci M. Rose

Kaci M. Rose writes steamy small town cowboys. She also writes under Kaci Rose and there she writes wounded military heroes, giant mountain men, sexy rock stars, and even more there. Connect with her below!

Website

Facebook

Kaci Rose Reader's Facebook Group

Goodreads

Book Bub

Join Kaci M. Rose's VIP List (Newsletter)

More Books by Kaci M. Rose

The Cowboy and His Christmas Rockstar – Savannah and Ford

The Cowboy and His Billionaire – Brice and Kayla

Walker Lake, Texas

The Cowboy and His Beauty - Sky and Dash

About Kaci M Rose

Kaci M Rose writes cowboy, hot and steamy cowboys set in all town anywhere you can find a cowboy.

She enjoys horseback riding and attending a rodeo where is always looking for inspiration.

Kaci grew on a small farm/ranch in Florida where they raised cattle and an orange grove. She learned to ride a four-wheeler instead of a bike (and to this day still can't ride a bike) and was driving a tractor before she could drive a car.

Kaci prefers the country to the city to this day and is working to buy her own slice of land in the next year or two!

Kaci M Rose is the Cowboy Romance alter ego of Author Kaci Rose.

See all of Kaci Rose's Books here.

the USA
town, DE
mber 2022

Made
Midd
11 Dec